L

TOUGH COMPANY

Walt Bender was a renegade from Texas who had been hired by a Mexican outfit to head up a war against the sheepmen. He thought he could tame the gringo herders, but how could he manage to tame the boss's daughter who wouldn't think twice about knifing a man?

Walt Bender was charged with murder and called a coward, but he was determined to prove everyone wrong.

Clem Colt was a pseudonym of **Nelson Nye** who was born in Chicago, Illinois. He was educated in schools in Ohio and Massachusetts and attended the Cincinnati Art Academy. His early journalism experience was writing publicity releases and book reviews for the *Cincinnati Times-Star* and the *Buffalo Evening News*. In 1935 he began working as a ranch hand in Texas and California and became an expert on breeding quarter horses on his own ranch outside Tucson, Arizona. Much of this love for horses can be found in exceptional novels such as *Wild Horse Shorty* and *Blood of Kings*. He published his first Western short story in *Thrilling Western* and his first Western novel in 1936. He continued from then on to write prolifically, both under his own name and the bylines Drake C. Denver and Clem Colt. During the Second World War, he served with the U.S. Army Field Artillery. In 1949–1952 he worked as horse editor for *Texas Livestock Journal*. He was one of the founding members of the Western Writers of America in 1953 and served twice as its president. His first Golden Spur Award from the Western Writers of America came to him for best Western reviewer and critic in 1954. In 1958–1962 he was frontier fiction reviewer for the *New York Times Book Review*. His second Golden Spur came for his novel *Long Run*. His virtues as an author of Western fiction include a tremendous sense of authenticity, an ability to keep the pace of a story from ever lagging, and a fecund inventiveness for plot twists and situations. Some of his finest novels have had off-trail protagonists such as *The Barber of Tubac*, and both *Not Grass Alone* and *Strawberry Roan* are notable for their outstanding female characters. His books have sold over 50,000,000 copies worldwide and have been translated into the principal European languages. The *Los Angeles Times* once praised him for his "marvelous lingo, salty humor, and real characters." Above all, a Nye Western possesses a vital energy that is both propulsive and persuasive.

TOUGH COMPANY

Clem Colt

GUNSMOKE

First published by Wright and Brown.

This hardback edition 2004
by BBC Audiobooks Ltd
by arrangement with
Golden West Literary Agency

ISBN 0 7540 8278 4

British Library Cataloguing in Publication Data available.

Printed and bound in Great Britain by
Antony Rowe Ltd., Chippenham, Wiltshire

CONTENTS

1 | BLUE ROAN RUNNING

OBSCURITY was what Walt Bender was hunting when he climbed up out of the desert's white glare and found this wild tangle of greenery before him. There was a dilapidated shack half buried in the pines where he could rest for awhile and get the saddle kinks out of him and a heap of new grass to pad out the ribs of that stout-hearted horse which had moved him eighty miles on a hatful of water.

They were travel worn and weary and there was no real reason, so far as he could see, why they shouldn't hole up here. This was a homesteader's claim and long abandoned by the look of it, the warped door hanging open, the rusted stovepipe drunkenly canted and the cleared land before it grown to crab grass and jimson. It made a picture of futility not many would have cared for, but Bender was in a mood to find any place suitable which had no star-packers cluttering the scenery.

He was a bleak-eyed man with sun-blackened cheeks and a mass of yellow hair sweatily plastered across his forehead. This was how the reward bills showed him, and if you didn't want trouble you had better sheer away because he was all done with running. Six solid months he'd been pushed by tin badges, driven from his ranch, turned away from jobs and people—and all because of a whittle whanging sidewinder who didn't care no more about dropping a politician than he would about finding worms in his biscuits.

Naturally the dodgers said nothing of that. They said WANTED FOR MURDER in boldfaced caps; that was how Lasham had framed him for being too damned fond of his grass. Had

1

it been anyone less than old Toby Bronsen the fat slob couldn't have cut it, but Toby had been a state's senator and no one could see how the sheep crowd could profit by killing the goose which had laid all their eggs—no one, that is, but Walt Bender. And who was going to listen to a fool caught red-handed with a gun in his fist while Lasham bellowed "Grab him!" at the top of his lungs?

He'd got away from that crowd by the skin of his teeth and was still on the dodge, Lasham managing that adroitly.

"Sheep killer" was what Lasham called him, and "cold turkey" was another of the vinegarroon's pet names which the sheep pool took up and hung onto him. If there was any one man in that West Texas country Walt Bender would sure like to blast into dollrags, that feller was Lasham. Deef Lasham who had tossed Walt aside like he wasn't no more than a chunk of waste paper. Lasham who, loud in front of the packed mob attending that rally, had called him "a damn exterminatin' son of a bitch!"

And the hell of it was Bender hadn't killed anyone—he'd been just a white chip in a no-limit game. But a thing like that can work on a man.

It had been working on Bender.

Every time he had run into another of those handbills Lasham's hirelings had scattered from Grandfalls to Canutillo the crazy tightness in his head had got tighter, the volcanic rage inside him a little nearer to tearing loose.

Oh, they'd been cute, all right—they'd been slicker than slobbers with never a sign of a broadsheet before him so long as he'd kept his horse pointing west. But let him turn north, let him lope awhile south or try to cut back east, and there were those handbills flaunting his likeness from tree, post and outhouse.

And that was how he'd been closed out of Texas.

The line was forty miles behind him, across the damn blow holes and that white hell of desert, beyond the green spikes of the sentinel yuccas. Ahead lay the West Potrillos, their upthrust peaks showing over the pines in a high ragged sweep of broken blues and purples against the bright rim of the dying sun. Not exactly a promised land perhaps, but one at least not likely to be overrun with lawmen.

Manyanner land, the Texicans called it, a place where one day was much the same as another and nobody cared where the hell a man came from so long as he did not upset cherished customs. A land permeated with the hush of past centuries, where traditions were honored and the nights were made gay with guitars and laughing lips and only mission bells told the careless passage of time.

And so to hell with Texas—let the damned sheep have it!

NIGHT was crowding the shank of evening when Bender's roan crossed the level and moved in toward the shack. He was almost abreast the swaybacked roof of the porch when a shot ripped a startling hole through the stillness.

Bender's eyes turned narrow and he held the horse quiet, hearing the echoes of that report strike and shatter against stone. It had come, he decided, from somewhere beyond and to the left of the building. And then he heard brush break beneath a fast traveling body and maneuvered the gelding around the shack very quietly, again sitting motionless with hand outstretched to choke off at once any sound from the animal.

Now he heard horses move with a rush to the right, their hoofs soft-drumming through the aisles of the pines, coming steadily nearer; and he moved again.

Full dark came suddenly and, with an equal abruptness, very shortly thereafter three horsemen burst from the pines and tore past, traveling south.

Bender felt the call of this night, of this wilderness, not wanting the smallest part in this business but not wanting, either, to go off with the thought of somebody dying because he hadn't had guts enough to go to their aid.

He listened to the three who had passed roar away in the darkness and he put the roan into movement, thinking to go through the pines and perhaps find what the score was. Certainly the shot had come from over there someplace, from some ravine or gulch.

He found it black, black almost as ink, drifting through

the aisles of these lofty pines. He kept thinking about the report of that shot, about the way it had sounded, the suddenness and the finality of it, and the uncaring rush of that later departure. Almost it had sounded like a bushwhacking.

Because the gelding's hoofs were making very little sound on this matted covering Bender had thought several times to catch the rumor of something. Now he heard it distinctly, the strike of iron on stone, and his mind translated this into an approaching rider, his analysis of the sound convincing him the man was coming off a rim. Now a rim to Bender meant a gulch or canyon and this tied in nicely with his earlier thought that the shot he had heard might have come from such a place. Was this the one who had fired it or the one who'd been fired at?

It might be just as well, he decided, to let the fellow work past without realizing his presence. Accordingly he stopped. But the man didn't seem to be in any great hurry. It was his mount, by the sound, who was picking the footing. He did a considerable amount of stopping which could indicate, of course, the cropping of grass. Except that grass didn't usually grow well on stone. Bender reckoned he could chalk those pauses up to nerves on the part of the rider. The guy was feeling edgy and was doing a lot of listening.

He was, Bender figured, perhaps a hundred yards ahead of him, a little over on the right and still traveling in rock. When the hoofs stopped again there was sound on Bender's left, also ahead of him, though more nearly on a level. It was horse sound, it was closer and it was also moving nearer.

Cursing under his breath, Bender wished he'd had the wit to have stayed out of these trees. There were others moving up behind him now and to move at all would be to court discovery.

The man off the wall abruptly raised his voice. "See anything?"

"Nothin' round the shack," one of the group behind Bender said. "Think we better try combin' that canyon, Art?"

The man to the left and ahead of Bender said, "Who fired?"

Bender was beginning to feel acutely his lack of knowledge of this region.

When no one answered Art's question about the shot, Art said, "Did anyone get hit?"

But no one answered that, either. The group behind Bender now began to move up and, perforce, Bender also moved, but much more slowly, much more carefully. Somebody said, "If he come this far he must have gone into the canyon unless he struck for the desert."

"He wouldn't do that," Art said, "if he could help it. We'd have him cut off if he went into the desert."

"I ain't so sure about that," one of the others objected. "He's bound to know we mean business. He may have decided this deal ain't worth dyin' for."

Another said impatiently: "If he went into the canyon he may slip out the other end—"

"No danger of that," Art said. "I've got Curly and Beans and Spuds Moran over there just waitin' for him to show his damn face."

Those behind him were getting nearer Bender now; the first man wasn't more than a horse length away. His rifle, like Bender's, was laying across his saddle. Bender now swung left to go around a tree and was sorely tempted to keep right on going only he knew he'd never make it. Riding with the group was one thing, riding away from it something else. He took only long enough to let that first man get ahead of him, then he came around the tree and paired off with another who was just a black shape in this gloom beneath the pines.

They came out of the trees in the next twenty feet and it was too late then for him to drop aside. The dark maw of the canyon opened directly ahead of them and he caught a vague look at the man who'd come off the wall.

Another dimseen shape trotted up from the left and this was Art, Bender guessed, checking his mount with the rest. This bunch was all about him now, choking the canyon's mouth with their horses, milling around in restless movement yet too close in their jingling and creaking to suit him. He tugged his hatbrim lower and bent forward in the saddle, reaching down as though to take the slack out of the roan's front girth.

"I keep thinkin'," Art said, "about that shot. Uncommon odd, I call it, with the whole crew scourin' round here that none of you'll admit to knowin' anything about it. That damn gun never fired itself!"

A man three horses away said, "What the hell? That stinkin' tomale prob'ly let off his pistol. He's been jumpy enough or he'd not have cut over this way in the first place."

"Would a *mozo* risk givin' himself away like that?" Art's voice turned rougher, the violence of his thinking getting into it now. "Forty-five hundred's a big chunk of money, more than some of you gents'll ever make in a lifetime."

All the horsemen around Bender sat still now. The head of his roan was against a dun's shoulder. A yard away on his right a pair of riders faced toward him and a man on his left had his knee against Bender's. If one of this bunch should decide to strike a match . . .

"You know what I think?" Art abruptly demanded. "I think one of you brush poppers come up with that feller. I think one of you slick sons got the bright notion of gettin' hands on that dough an' then rollin' your cotton."

"That," cried the man on Bender's left, "is a hell of a thing to say, Art!"

"I'm sayin' it. And I'll tell you something else. I better not come onto that pepper-gut's body and not find no damn dough in his pockets." He let them digest that and then he said quietly. "Chuck, I want you up on that north rim again. I'll take the south and the rest of you rannies spread out and comb all the brush in that canyon—and what I mean, *work* at it. If this peckerneck gets back to the ranch with that dinero it's goin' to be too damn bad for somebody. Now get at it!"

A lean gap in their ranks showed now just behind Bender and he backed the roan into it, swerving him then to round the man on his right. His leg brushed roughly against that one's leg and the man growled sharply, "For Christ's sake Joe, have you got your damn eyes shut?" And a man up ahead of him wheeled, saying, "What?" And the first one's head twisted round to look at Bender. He said, "Wait a minute, bucko," but Bender kept going, sliding the roan in between two passing others and cutting back of them to edge around a third and stay with this man awhile.

Glancing back across his shoulder Bender saw the one he'd locked knees with yank his horse out of line and sit there blackly waiting for the three last riders to pass him. In a minute, Bender knew, this one was going to be coming after him, and he tried to make his mind up. He wanted like hell to run but knew very well that the instant he did he'd have this whole damn push piling after him.

Just then the two men directly before him passed into the canyon's black obscurity, the heavier darkness swallowing them; and, with one quick look at that man coming up, Bender sent his own mount into this murk, shortening the length of the gelding's stride until the man who'd been siding him pulled ahead. Then he went with cocked muscles across the front of the drag, letting the roan drift a further ten paces till he had the low face of the south wall before him, there stopping.

Slipping his Winchester back in its scabbard, he pulled the blue neckerchief up to his eyes and again turned the roan till it was pointed as the others, holding the animal there without motion. His intention was to wait till the rest of this outfit moved deeper into the gulch, but the man who'd been hunting him was still plainly at it and now this one's voice, climbing over the riding sounds, cried: "Chuck! There's—"

"Button your lip!" Chuck slammed back at him wickedly. "If you ain't got no more sense than to go shoutin' names—"

"Hold on," Art called. "What's the matter down there?"

Bender, against the wall, was now unable to see any of them, but he could hear the low grumble of exchanged comments, the restless milling of horses, spur sound and bit sound.

Through the felted blackness the hunter's dissatisfied voice rose again. "There's a stray down here someplace. I think that spik's with us—"

"I think you're crazy," Art said, "but we'll damn quick find out. Don't any of you move from his tracks till I tell you. Chuck, move your horse up that wall twenty paces."

The sound of Chuck's horse came down plainly to Bender. If they were fixing to count noses he didn't think it would tell them much, now that he had got himself out of their way. He thought a light might do it if they could get a light strong enough, but if he'd judged this bunch right they weren't going to be wanting to have their mugs seen.

"Okey," Chuck called.

"One at a time now," Art said, "you rannies down there step your broncs up ten paces. As each man moves forward he will give his name clearly, then hold his horse quiet till he gets recognition, thereafter settin' still till we get this thing done with. You in the lead now—move up."

Bender grinned in the dark, hearing the first man go forward. "Jid," this one said, and Chuck called for another. There was horse sound again and a different voice: "Ed." A third rider moved up but before he could speak there came a sudden wild clatter of metal on rock. It seemed to come from beyond them, deeper into the gulch, both okeyed men firing instantly. Sound battered monstrously against the stone cliffs, clattering down and around them in shattering fragments. Through this came curses, shouted questions, more sound piled on sound as saddle guns drove unseen lead through the uproar. One man's yell went racketing above it and a sudden concerted rushing of riders flung hoof thunder into the tumult.

Bender whirled his roan and, clinging flattened against its side, sent it streaking in the direction of the pines he had so recently come out of. The barrel-toned roar of Art's angry orders was almost submerged in the bedlam behind him and somewhere a horse gave one scream of great agony.

What it was which had startled that bunch into firing Bender did not know, nor did he give it much thought. He was directing all his attention toward getting out of this gulch with his scalp still in place if there was any chance of doing it. He might have got clear right then except that all of this bunch hadn't lost their heads.

He had the roan gelding pushed to its limit when they crashed head-on into the rump of another which appeared to be bound in the same direction. A girl's frightened cry came out of the blackness and was instantly lost in the scream of her pony as the force of collision hurled it onto its knees. Bender's own horse managed to stay on its feet but was flung half around, throwing Bender's masked face full into the glare of an exploding pistol. He felt the heat of that blast and tossed away in that moment of lifting temper the caution which thus far had kept these guns off him.

He lifted the Winchester out of its scabbard and struck with it, club like, the brought-around barrel beating breath from a man who fell off his horse backwards. Gripping hard with his knees Bender pulled himself upright, sliding the saddlegun back in its sheath and reaching—sheer reflex—for the butt of his pistol.

It was lucky he did, for another dark rider was driving straight at him, already so close Walt could see the pale blob of his face in the starlight. Gigging the roan to one side as the fellow lashed past Bender hammered the back of his head with the beltgun.

Then he flung the roan forward. "Where are you—where are you?"

"Here!" cried the girl, and she sprang from the shadows.

Kicking a boot from the stirrup he gave her his hand. She came up sure and swift, being dressed like a man, settling lightly behind him with a *"Madre de Dios!"* He felt her hands clutch his belt. He felt her lips at his ear. "Through the trees," she cried softly, "and be quick or we'll die here."

He spurred the roan toward the pines while behind them a gun laid flat crashes of sound through the canyon. Yet loud as this was Bender heard Art bellow. "Drop them, you fools! Cut them down—cut them down!" Almost instantly then the voice of a rifle began to break up the night with its crack-crack-crack chatter.

Bender crouched just as low as he could get in the saddle, feeling the girl's body crowding ever tighter against him, raking the gelding's wet flanks with his spurs. But the horse didn't have the reach he'd had that morning. Those grueling hours in the desert had taken their toll and this girl's added weight was not helping. The horse was doing its best but its wind was a racking in-and-out rush of sound and it was moving stiff-legged in what was almost a stagger.

Bender heard those blue whistlers singing closer and closer but he still thought they'd make it and get into the pines when something went *thwut* and the gelding broke stride. He didn't quit, he kept going but he was losing momentum.

Bender groaned when the horse began to fall apart under them.

"We're goin' to have to get off."

"Yes," the girl said. She took her hands off his belt and was gone on the instant. Bender felt like a deserter pulling his boots from the stirrups. He hauled up one leg, patted the gelding and jumped.

2 | THE SUDDEN TURN

THEY plunged into the trees, Bender striving to follow the elusive shape of the girl, wondering how she'd got into this trap, wondering if she were the one with the money. He could smell the dry mold being kicked up by bullets and he could hear other bullets droning viciously around him, ripping bark off the pines and squealing in ricochet. He'd grabbed the rifle off the roan when he had jumped, and still had it; but he didn't feel at all inclined to stop right now and use it.

That lead-slinging bunch had been looking for a man, but the girl's clothes might have fooled them—not, Bender thought, that it was like to make much difference if she were the one who was packing that dinero. He didn't have to see faces to know these men's kind. He'd met gun-hung drifters of their stripe before and understood very clearly how much mercy could be expected by a woman at their hands. It was the only reason he tagged after this girl against every impulse of experience and judgment.

He believed they would both have a much better chance of getting clear if they split up now, but he did not offer this thought to the girl. He was too curious, for one thing, and his pride would not permit him to put forward a suggestion which might seem, if later repeated, a disparagement of his manhood. But he could not help reflecting they weren't being very smart. Afoot they would be lucky even to get as far as that shack which at best, as Bender saw it, would be damned indifferent shelter.

The trees by now were beginning to make an effective screen against the guns. Panting, Bender called to the girl and she waited for him to come up with her. While he was still trying to catch enough breath for his question they heard a rush of horses and the girl caught his hand. "We must get to the house—"

"We can't stand them off there for—"

"Please!"

Bender shrugged. "All right," he said grimly, not seeing that it made much difference. If dying in that shack would make her feel happier it was okey with him because they'd sure as hell die if they remained in these pines. Art wouldn't make the same mistake twice; it was plain by their sound that he had spread his men out to where not even a rabbit would elude them this time.

They broke out of the trees and saw the shack's bulk before them. He followed the girl across the creaking porch and dragged the door shut behind them. He felt her hand on his arm guiding him over to a window. "There is where they will have to come out. Try to hold them off a little while with your rifle."

She moved away from him then, her spurred heels crossing the floor with a deal more confidence than Bender could feel. "You have a gun?" he asked.

"Not any more. I threw it away to distract their attention. Have you plenty of shells for your rifle?"

"About a dozen, I think—"

"Then you must make each one count."

She was the coolest dame he had ever bumped into.

Make them count. Bender grinned. You could trust him for that. He had no more desire to be killed than the next guy. "You better get down an' stay flat on the floor."

His eyes got blurry peering into the gloom and he closed them a moment, hearing her busily scraping at something with her foot. He wondered who she was, how she'd got into this business, and asked her if she had the money they were hunting.

She admitted she had. She said, "I'm going to try and hide it. Hold them off as long as you can and don't be afraid of killing them. They are Chesseldine's men—that was him they called 'Art'."

He heard her grunt, heard the squeak of strained boards, and then he dropped behind the window and cuddled the Winchester to his shoulder, thrusting its barrel across the sill. Where he heard the girl's breath there was a flat slap of sound as though of something heavy falling, and he twisted his head, calling out, "Are you all right?"

"Yes," she said, panting. "Let me worry with this. You watch out for those cow thieves and don't waste your cartridges."

At the edge of the pines Bender caught a blur of motion but he held his fire, waiting as she'd suggested till he could make his shots count. He said softly, "Who's Chesseldine?"

"He is suspected of being the leader of all the stock thieves around here. He calls himself a speculator in cattle and pretends to be a great friend of my father who is very simple about such things. He stopped by our ranch two weeks ago and told my father the government was throwing open two hundred thousand acres of—"

The report of Bender's rifle crashed through the shack, obscuring her words; and just in front of the place where the pines loomed blackest a running man threw up his hands and pitched headlong. "Down!" Bender cried, and dropped flat himself as the answering fire of Chesseldine's men hammered the boards of the wall with their bullets, some of these tearing all the way through the shack. The smell of dust rose up and mingled with the acrid stench of black powder.

When the men in the pines dropped back to reload Bender kicked out a short length of rotten board near the floor and, stretched prone, thrust the barrel of his rifle through this and waited. "You all right?" he called again to the girl.

"Yes. There's an old root cellar beneath a trap in the floor. I've hidden the money—"

"You stay down there," Bender said, and then, after a moment of closely watching the pines, "How'd they get onto this forty-five hundred?"

"Chesseldine said we could bid in the grass nearest us— about eight thousand acres—for that amount of money. My father said we didn't have that amount and Chesseldine said he knew a man who would lend it. He said this man knew my father's reputation and if we cared to fill out a paper he left with us we could see this man in Columbus on the twentieth and he would let us have the money."

"The twentieth was yesterday—"

"Yes. My father sent his foreman—"

"How did *you* get hold of the money?"

"When I read the small print on the paper we were to sign, I told my father the loan would be secured by a mortgage on Tres Pinos—that is the name of our ranch. He said no matter. But I did not like for him to sign this paper, even though I knew we had the need of more grass. My mother, of course, would say nothing; when I tried to tell a little of what I thought my father became very angry and signed it. So then he sent his foreman to Columbus for the money. But something," she said, putting a hand to her breast, "came to warn me against these Greeks bearing gifts—"

"Greeks? You mean," said Bender, startled, "this Chessy guy's—"

"Oh, no—a figure of speech only. They are Americans, of course—of a very low type. But I became extremely suspicious:

for, consider: this Chesseldine, who even among the gringos has a poor reputation, comes directly to my father to speak about this grass. I ask myself why this should be so; and, when my father says he does not have so much money, is it reasonable for this man who speaks of Mexicans as 'greasers' to know already of another generous *Norte Americano* who will advance my father the price of this grass? And the date! This so-generous man will be in Columbus only on the twentieth —could we be indeed so fortunate?"

"Yeah. I see what you mean," Bender nodded. "But I thought this bunch talked like they were expectin' a Mexican——"

"My father's foreman is Mexican. His name is Pedro Gonzales."

"So you went instead."

"No. It was all settled that Pedro should go for this money. Chesseldine said he would arrange for it to be given to no one but Pedro. After Pete left, I made the excuse to go and visit a friend who lives at Afton. Instead of the provisions that were placed in my saddlebags I took these clothes—a foolish thing."

"But the money?" Bender said, twisting around to try and see her.

"I waited along the *Camino Primativo,* about three hundred *metros* beyond the town's last house. When I saw my father's foreman I rode out of the brush and called him. He was very annoyed when he saw who I was. I thought at first the man had not given him the money, expecting to see a great sack on his saddle. But he said he had got it, that they'd given it in paper which he had in a belt underneath his shirt. I told him I would take it, that I felt sure he was going to be robbed of this money. He made a great deal of talk but in the end gave it over—"

A sudden thunder of hoofbeats cut into her words and Bender, cursing, whirled back to his peephole but they were already past where he could fire from the floor. "Git flat," he growled angrily, and was jumping toward the gray square of the window when that wall of the shack began to rattle like a drum. Something tore past his hip and went *chunk!* in the back wall, and Bender flung up his Winchester and fired where he was.

He heard the thin whine as a slug cuffed his hat-brim and the instant *thwut* of it striking the wall. The thunder of Chesseldine's riders swept past and was muted a little as they cut back toward the trees. Bullets still crashed into the boards of the shack and he could tell where they were by the side these were striking.

That rush had been to test him, to find out how well this shack would be defended. The next time they came they'd rush this place in real earnest. He told the girl: "You'd better run for it. Crawl out that back door and duck into the lean-to. While they're rushing this side try to make those east trees an' keep—"

"Ride right into it this time!"

A round blast of flame leaped out of the pines and someone commenced a high rebel yelling. As Bender flung himself flat to get away from that lead he heard a second rush of horses tear out of the timber. He came onto one knee and ripped a slug through that blackness, continuously firing until his rifle clicked empty. He heard the girl come crawling across to his side and she caught up the Winchester, saying, "Give me your cartridges."

He wanted to tell her to get back in that hole but there was no use in that once he'd used his last bullet; they'd come after her then and how the hell could he stop them? He gave her what he had and then crouched back on his haunches. He lifted his pistol, waiting till he saw the dark shapes of Art's riders swing hellity larrup across the front of the yard, laying his quick fire through a corner of the window. Lead ripped splinters of wood from the sill and other slugs batted the wall all around him. He fired again, putting two shots into that huddle of riders. A horse went down and the rest swept over him. Another rider reared up and went off his mount screaming.

Bender dropped his dry gun and took the reloaded Winchester. "You've got five shells, that's all," she said and, fumbling at his belt, began reloading the sixshooter.

Bender laid the barrel of the rifle across the sill. He took one quick look and crashed out four slugs as fast as he could trigger. One horse went up on its hind legs, pawing, toppling backwards square in the path of another. One was so close when Bender's slug struck, it smashed sideways into the corner of the building, flinging its rider clear across the porch, stopping with its head and one leg through the wall. Chesseldine's crew broke and scattered, Bender dropping one more as they raced for the trees.

"Close," he grunted, sleeving sweat from his eyes. "You should have gone when I told you. They won't try that again. They'll be coming for us afoot now, creepin' an' crawlin' from all sides at once."

He thought to see her shake her head but in this gloom he wasn't sure. "I think," she told him soberly, "the odds will be in favor of their going away—"

"Without that dough?" Bender stared at her pityingly. He thought anyone exhibiting that kind of faith must be either very young or in line for a string of spools. He'd been through some close shaves and had sometimes wondered what shape the end might take but had never imagined himself boxed in a shack getting ready to die with an unknown woman.

He thrust a hand across the loops of his brush-clawed shell belt, finding them entirely devoid of live cartridges. Art's gun throwers, he thought, were probably injuning up now. They'd be a little more careful on this trip he reckoned; and abruptly remembered the man who'd been flung across the porch. If he could get that guy's cartridges. . . .

The girl said through the darkness, "You probably think I'm a fool to believe they'll go without the money, but you're forgetting they expected to encounter little trouble. They planned this very carefully as Chesseldine plans everything. The man's a coyote, not a wolf—"

"But the stake," said Bender drily, "is forty-five hundred dollars and around this kind of country that's a hell of a lot of money."

"And little good to him if he's caught."

"But who's to catch him?" Bender asked skeptically, "out here forty miles from nowhere?"

"This house is on my father's ranch. It belonged to a man who was sick in his chest whom my father permitted to live here. This robber knows as well as I how near he is to my father's *casa*. He knew that when he planned this thing. He had to get close because three trails come together just above these pines and he had to wait there or risk missing his quarry. It was expected to be simple—one shot, one dead body and away with our money. But I did not keep to the trail and now he's done too much shooting. He will be afraid to wait longer."

"How far off is your house?"

"Hardly over two miles by the trail; actually nearer. Already our *vaqueros* will be mounted and riding."

"They could still be too late." Bender lifted his head and took a look through the window. He was not reassured. "What's to prove they would have heard—"

"How could they help? Sound does curious things around here. The gallery of my father's *casa* faces this place and picks up many rumors, but I have more proof than that. When this sick man would get bad he would always fire his pistol and my mother would fix the herb medicine for him—"

"This bunch might not know that." Bender was willing to admit. Art might be getting a little nervous after all that firing, but he didn't believe the man was ready to ride off and say goodbye to that dinero. He had already shown himself contemptuous of Mexicans and, from the girl's talk, it would seem the whole Three Pines crew was chile-eaters. They were the best damn cowboys in the world and Bender knew it, but there were plenty of so-called white men in this region who professed to believe Mexicans were a cowardly lot who had no rights at all. And, from what he'd seen and heard, he imagined Art was of this persuasion.

"Let's just figure for the moment that we ain't out of this yet. One of them horses I shot threw a guy across the porch. On the chance he's got some shells I'm goin' to slip out there."

"I'll go with you—"

"You'll stay right where you are," Bender said to her sharply. "You may be figurin' this right, and I sure hope you are, but you're not setting foot outside of this shack until I'm convinced that bunch has gone diggin' for the tules."

It never occurred to Bender she might ignore his orders. He paused a moment to unlatch his gut hooks and then commenced crawling across the littered floor. He had not heard the girl close the trap but he knew he was on it when he felt the boards give a little under his weight. He thought the root cellar a damn poor place for that money but, considering the girl's convictions, he reckoned that at a pinch it might perhaps serve her purpose. His main interest right now was in gaining replacements for the loads in his pistol.

He saw the black hole of the doorless rear exit as a more solid oblong of the darkness before him, and moved up to it cautiously, stopping when he reached it to listen intently. He heard nothing which alarmed him nor did he hear any sound of the Three Pines *vaqueros.* As he had supposed, this doorway opened directly into the lean-to. The lean-to's open side, he remembered, faced east and was about two yards from that corner of the shack. The thrown rider, as near as Bender could figure, should be about the same distance from the corner at the opposite side; and the end of the shack around which he'd have to crawl was the farthest removed from the bunch who were bent on stopping his clock. Which was no proof, of course, that they had not changed position.

He debated the advisability of drawing his pistol, well aware if it were needed it would be needed mighty quick. But he decided to leave it in its sheath on his belt; there was too much risk, in his hand, of the stars striking up a gleam which might betray him.

The deep gloom of the shed closed around him like the smothering folds of a pure-black blanket. To the left and before him this murk was complete. To his right, along the house wall, night made a patterned wedge of blue shadows. Still on all fours, Bender pointed himself toward this and moved forward.

Bit by cautious bit he worked nearer, muscles tight and pulses pounding. He kept his face geared down, trying to pick a quiet way through an accumulated litter of discarded junk, finally reaching the opening and moving out of the shed.

It seemed to him at once as though a thousand eyes were watching. He was, in that moment, a cold and wholly desperate man who had counted his chances and accepted the risk; and then a low wind drifted across his face from the pines and he jerked up his head with both ears cocked, suddenly stopping.

He'd have sworn he'd caught the close-by breaking of a stick, and the skin at the base of his scalp began to prickle as he plowed the shadows with a widened wicked stare.

For frozen moments time stood still; then Bender's hand came off his gun butt and his shape recommenced its crawling and came against the wall's east corner.

Here the bulked ragged black of the pines came within twenty yards of him and he heard the tumult of his heart as he paused there, briefly listening.

Expecting any moment to hear the crash and bang of gunfire he dropped flat on his belly and commenced a forward wriggling meant to take him round the corner. He moved an arm, the opposite knee, and thought in that split second to catch the faroff sound of hurrying hoofs; in the next all thought was swept completely out of him as the fingers of his left extended forward-reaching hand, going round the building's angle, suddenly brushed and gripped another hand, gun-weighted, moving toward him.

3 | ONE FOR THE
| BOOK

SOME gents would do a world of thinking with their hand that way on another guy's wrist. Bender did not think at all. He flung all the weight he could get on that dewclaw, grinding it into the gravelly ground, banging it hard as he could against the house wall, then taking it with him as he rolled round the corner.

The gun went off, gouting flame past Walt's face, hammering the night with its tumultuous thunder; and then Walt was over him, pinning the man's middle with the weight of his body while muzzle light cut its streaks of yellow and purple against the black shapes of the shaggy pines. The man writhed like a snake, snarling curses and panting, as lead from those rifles beat against the shack wall, but Bender wouldn't let go. He rode the man's struggles as he'd ride a bad bronc, piling pressure on pressure as he forced that arm upward behind the man's twisted head until he heard bone grate.

The man screamed and went limp. Scooping up the dropped pistol, Bender unlatched the man's belt, buckling it about his own lean hips, half straightening then and hanging fire for a moment, not liking to leave this fellow so exposed. But he did, after all, because just then he heard the horses—heard them coming through the timber on a hard and lifting run.

Not caring to be trapped where he'd have no chance Bender dived around the corner, colliding with surprise against a crouched shape hurrying toward him. He damn near put a slug through the girl before he realized who this was he had hold of. He felt the strike of her heart against his ribs. Spurred then by anger, pushing her roughly into the shed, he said: "I thought I told you to stay inside—"

"But I was afraid you were hurt. I. . . ." He felt her shape stiffen. She cried, "Listen—the *vaqueros!* I told you they would come!" She would have gone running out there if Bender hadn't stopped her, forgetful of flying lead and everything else in her excitement.

But it was plain she had the right of it. Rifles were crashing all through the pines and there was a lot of wild yelling, the sound of the guns growing steadily more remote as the crew from the ranch strung out after the bushwhackers trying to fight clear through the black of that canyon.

"You're hurting me," she said, and he let go of her shoulder.

He scowled in an embarrassed silence. Then he said to her

gruffly, "Better get in there an' dig up your money while we're waitin'. When your crew gets back I'll be rockin' along."

He stepped out of the shed and went back around the corner, thinking to have a closer look at that fellow who he believed was the man that had been flung across the porch. But the man was no longer lying there.

Bender roved a hard glance through the roundabout shadows, then crouched and looked again. He couldn't believe any fellow with an out-of-whack shoulder was going to be able to get very far and, with this thought in his mind, carefully combed the whole clearing, still without finding him. Thoroughly unconvinced, he cruised into the pines but finally gave it up. The guy might not have spilled his guts anyway.

When he came back to the cabin the girl said, "I'm ready."

"For what?" Bender asked.

"Why, to go home, of course. Did you think I'd planned to camp here all night?"

"Your crew will be back——"

"I've had enough of this place."

She gave him that news as a queen might have spoken. Bender scrinched his eyes, scowling. "I ain't too partial about it myself, but we don't have no horses and trampin' two miles with a hull on each shoulder is more than I'm engagin' to care for right now."

"One of the crew will pick up your saddle when he comes after mine in the morning."

"Maybe I won't be around in the morning."

"Maybe you won't, but unless you like walking you'll have to come to Tres Pinos to get hold of a horse." She eyed him a moment. "You may as well come with me."

"I'll get a horse from your crew."

"If you wait for the crew you'll be more apt to get a bullet. They'll think you're one of that crowd they've been chasin——"

"I'll chance that."

"You've no need to. Why must you be so stubborn?" she asked angrily. "It would be different if you were bound somewhere else, but you're not. You're going to pass the ranch anyway——"

"Where'd you get that notion?"

"Didn't you come off the desert?"

"What's that got to do with it?"

"If you stay here awhile—"

"I'm not stayin'," he said impatiently; and he sure as hell wasn't. Not after that gun welcome he'd just gotten. The last thing he wanted was any more trouble.

She appeared to be trying to work out something. He could feel her eyes on him, saw the way she was canting her head as she watched him. "Perhaps not," she told him finally, "but I think you're mistaken."

"I'm leavin'," Bender said, "just as quick as I get a horse."

"Then you may as well see that I get home with this money. The nearest place you'll get a horse is at Tres Pinos. We raise nothing but the best. And if you should happen to admire one my father will insist on giving it to you."

Bender looked at her slanchways. "I'm scared that kind of horse would come too high," he told her drily.

She stood awhile not speaking but continuing to watch him, and then she remarked abruptly: "What you do with your life is, of course, your own business—but a man never got away from anything by running."

This girl's calm assumption of so cool an authority, quite as much as the way she'd pushed that last remark at him, stirred the cramped boil of temper that was smoldering in Bender; and he flung back at her sharply: "You're a sight too smart for your own good, missy."

Her small laugh was short and held an edge close to bitterness. "You are not the first Texican who has come up off that desert but you're cut to the pattern. 'Drifter' is what Cash Fentress would call you—meaning a man who is footloose and seeking new pastures. I am probably not as charitable as our estimable sheriff who came that way himself. I think you're a noose dodger. A man who's left Texas because he didn't dare stay."

Bender opened his mouth and clamped it wickedly shut while a wind off the peaks waved the tops of the pines.

"But don't let that bother you," she went on inexorably.

"My father's pride will not let him take advice from a woman. He'll welcome you as he has all the others who've come into these hills and now live off our cattle. To my father all strangers are brothers—especially gringos. He does not understand that only the no-good ones ever come to the Potrillos."

She quit talking to him then and moved a little way apart and Bender, bleak of eye, strode into the shack and put on his spurs. She did not speak as he passed her nor when he came out and went savagely tramping off into the pines.

He was back after a while with a saddle on his shoulder. "All right," he said in a curt tone of voice. "Which way?"

She led off without answering, moving into the timber. The stars were much brighter now and, over in the east beyond the tops of the mountains, the black sky showed a shining where the moon was coming up. Bender judged it was about ten.

They walked in a complete silence. She walked fast for a girl and, as the saddle got heavier, he would have been perfectly willing to have slowed down a bit, but he was damned if he would say so.

Presently he saw the lights of the ranch and reckoned her folks were waiting up for the outfit. The moon, now above the black shapes of the crags, threw a pattern of blue and silver across the steadily rising trail which made their travel much easier. Bender, at least, was able to quit stumbling although the pitch of the trail made a noise of his breathing which did little to improve the gravelled state of his mind.

Noose dodger!

He'd never been so set back in his life by a woman. Who the hell did she think she was, by godfreys!

They reached the top of the trail and came out on a table-land flat as a mesa. Tres Pinos looked huge in this bright flood of silver flung down by the moon. Typically Spanish, this layout was built like a fortress and looked near as vast, Bender thought with his glance taking in the great walls. There was a deep and dark gallery all across the part facing them, the posts supporting its roof big around as his waist.

Several *mozos* came hurrying out of the shadows, the girl quieting their hubbub with a few words in the lingo.

"We'll go in," she said, turning. "My father will wish to thank you—"

"He can keep his damn thanks. All I want is a horse."

"That can wait till the morning. My father would feel insulted were you to refuse to spend the night."

Swearing under his breath Bender followed her.

One of the *mozos* went hastening ahead of them and, as they stepped onto the gallery, flung open a great door. Lamplight, butter yellow, put a golden shine on the flagstones and, in this refracted glow, Bender saw that the girl was in the clothes of a charro. And then he'd followed her into the room and she was saying, "Papa mio, you are beholden to this man for the life of your so-disobedient daughter." And to Bender, "I would like for you to know my father, Don Leopoldo Jose Ramon Lopez y Gallardo, master of Tres Pinos."

Bender, looking across her shoulder, saw an old man stand, peer and start to come forward. He was tall for a Mexican and thick through the middle with a scraggle of whiskers curling out from his chin. He was dressed in a garb befitting a *ranchero* and there was gray in his hair and an air of unchallenged authority about him as his bright active eyes explored the stranger before him.

His voice, a rich baritone, was sincerity incarnate. "My house is yours," he said, smiling, and reached out a hand which the Texan took reluctantly.

"Mighty white of you," Bender said, "but a house ain't what I'm lookin' for. My name's Walt Bender. I'm fresh off the desert an'—like I told your fire-eatin' daughter—all I'm wantin' right now is a horse."

"You shall have the best one in my stables," declared Don Leo, at last releasing his hand. "But first will you not have a little coffee—some *frijoles* or, at least, a glass of wine with some cakes? The coffee was roasted by my wife herself, and the wine by a distinguished friend in Socorro. Eladio!"

He clapped his hands and at once a swarthy pock-marked

mozo came from an inner doorway and stood, hat in hand, awaiting his pleasure.

"Shall it be cakes and the *vino*," enquired the old man, "or *tortillas y frijoles?*"

"Whatever you say," grumbled Bender, impatiently, wanting nothing so much as to get the hell out of there. "I'm in a kind of a hurry, and if you'll sell me a horse—"

"Eh? But to be sure," smiled Don Leo. "Tomorrow you shall have the finest horse of my raising, but tonight you shall be my guest and sleep in the bed of my illustrious grandparent, who was man-at-arms to the Emperor Maximilian." He gave a few rapid orders in a kind of bastard Spanish and the *mozo* hurried off to attend them. "Will you wash, my friend?"

Looking round for the girl, Bender saw she was gone, so with a shrug he followed the old man into a large inner patio that was pleasant with shrubs and the sound of a fountain. There was an arcaded walk around the four sides of this and a kind of orange light was shed over the whole by eight wrought-iron lanterns hung from hooks placed at intervals in the logs which supported the walk's ramada-type roof. The whole center of this patio was open to the stars.

Bender followed Don Leo into a ten-by-twelve room whose dirt floor was freshly swept and recently sprinkled to keep the dust down. A gleaming mirror of hand-rolled glass framed by tin embossed with much workmanship hung above a chest of drawers on which were a wash basin and pitcher made of Indian-glazed pottery. The biggest share of the space was given over to a huge white four-poster with an image of the Virgin above it.

"Nice place," Bender said as he washed away the grime and combed his hair with his fingers. He picked up one of a stack of towels and dried himself, shook his shirt out the door and got into it again. He started to pick up his hat, caught the old man's expression and tossed it back in the chair.

"This will be your room for as long as you care to stay," pronounced the old man, smiling pleasantly. "We do not have too many strangers, but every man is welcome. Everything you see is at your disposal, and if there should be something which you want which is not at once apparent you have only to clap the hands and one of your servants will find it for you."

"I'm much obliged," Bender grunted, "but I must go in the morning. To tell you the truth, I'm in a sweat to reach . . . Deming," he said for lack of anything better.

Don Leo's eyes sharpened slightly but he was much too polite to make any remark which might be construed as a question. He led the way into a dining room and took a seat with his guest at the gleaming pine table where an old woman, her hair swathed in a *rebozo,* brought coffee, a tall stack of new-made tortillas and a giant-size olla of red beans cooked in chili. Bender attacked these with gusto for it was long since he'd eaten and the sight of this food made him ravenous.

When he had finished and was lifting his third cup of coffee, a man in a big hat stepped in off the patio, briefly scowled at the visitor and waited for Don Leo to notice him. He wore his big black sombrero on the back of his head and kept it in place by two straps of cured leather which passed under his chin and were secured by an engraved silver concha. He was incredibly thin and surprisingly redheaded with the skin of his face both florid and freckled.

Don Leo waited till Bender had put down his cup. "This is my foreman, Pedro Gonzales, who has grown from a boy at Tres Pinos," he explained. "Mr. Bender is spending the night with us, Pete, and tomorrow you will show him the best of our horses. He has business in Deming and will need a good mount."

Gonzales' face showed no interest. He said to the old man in Spanish: "I did not see Blanca but we found her dead horse and I have just been told she came home with this gringo. We followed those cow thieves through the canyon, not quitting till they got into the bad lands. Only four got away."

Also in Spanish the old man said, "I will talk of this tomorrow," and then, in English, "Let us go into the sala. Josefa will bring us the wine and little cakes."

They took chairs in the main room and, after they had been served by the old woman in the *rebozo,* Don Leo clapped his hands and told a servant to request the pleasure of his wife's and daughter's company.

Bender presently caught the tap-tap-tapping of a cane moving nearer along the flagged walk in the patio and the low murmur of feminine voices. He got to his feet when the ladies appeared, very conscious of the girl yet bowing gravely when Don Leo presented her mother. Dona Ruthena was small, a little angular and stooped, much fairer of complexion than her husband whose face was deeply bronzed from frequent contacts with the sun.

Bender noticed these things as he acknowledged her greeting, but mostly his attention was on the younger woman. He found it hard to reconcile his earlier conception with the extraordinary appearance of the girl now standing before them.

She wore a daring gown of bright red silk, but she wore it demurely and was amazingly proper, not speaking save when spoken to and revealing not the least sign of that bitterness with which she had called him a noose dodger or of that adamant spirit with which she'd advised him to make every one of his cartridges count.

Only by her voice would he have known her. It had the same husky cadence, the same precise inflection. The lamplight exhibited charms the night had hidden. She had a golden complexion that was in startling contrast to the appearance he had imagined. She had the narrow hips and astounding eyes of a creature stepped bodily from the best work of Villalbaso. She had hair that was black and black eyes, too, and a sultry, passionate look to her features that well matched the shape of her supple body. Grace seemed inherent in the least of her movements and, altogether, she was a great shock to Bender. He finally dragged his eyes off her and dropped into his chair where he did his best to ignore her.

It was not easy.

She moved with the lazy rhythm of a gypsy, with that slight sway of flank peculiar to women of Moorish blood. And, despite his intention, Bender found himself watching as she crossed to a couch and sat down beside her mother.

Don Leo said perplexedly, "I cannot think what we are to do with you, Blanca." He considered her with a worried frown plowing up the corrugations of his forehead. Then, turning to Bender, he asked apologetically if the Texan understood Spanish, smiling with real pleasure when Bender answered that he did. "Mostly, at Three Pines," he said, "it is our custom to speak the *Americano*, but sometimes it a little confuses me." He then asked in Spanish for his daughter to recount her experiences.

Blanca said, "First, papa mio, did you hear the sound of firing?"

When he said they had she did not look at Bender but he was not slow to get the point she was making. "Although he had just himself gotten home," said Don Leo, "Pete was certain you were in trouble and, although I did not believe any would offer you harm, when the firing became general at his insistence I allowed him to take the cowboys and look into it. And now, if you please, I would hear why you did this very foolish thing."

Blanca said she had been suspicious of Chesseldine's motives from the moment he had told Don Leo about the lease lands; that, after reading the paper which had to be signed to secure the loan, she had been more than ever convinced it was a plot of some kind designed to endanger her father's possession of Tres Pinos.

"But how could that be?" Don Leo protested.

"Have you not heard," she countered, "of such things happening to other ranches owned by Spanish-Americans? The Miraflores Ranch—"

"Is in the Burro Mountains," her father said testily, "where there is metal. There are no minerals at Tres Pinos. There is nothing here except land and cattle and too little grass at the moment for our own. The idea is fantastic!"

Bender did not say anything, although plainly the girl had been expecting his support. "Nevertheless," she said stubbornly, "I was convinced there was a plot and I am still of that opinion. I was chased. Men sought to rob me—"

"Of something Pedro shouldn't have given you," **Don Leo**

said, sternly eyeing his redheaded foreman. "If there was a plot it was against Pedro and not against you or myself or Tres Pinos. It is absurd to believe that a man who is kind enough to loan me money could possibly have any designs on this rancho—which he knows is not sufficient to support my own cattle."

"It is more unbelievable to *me*," she said half angrily, "that any drifter like Chesseldine should go out of his way to tell you of these grasslands and, when you say you haven't the money, to provide some man who will loan it. How did he know of this man? How, in the first place, did he learn that the American government would be throwing these Indian lands open to lease?"

"How can we know?" Don Leo said, plainly exasperated. "The *Norte Americanos* know many things about their government which a woman cannot understand. This does not make them any the less true. As for Mr. Chesseldine coming here and telling me about it, why indeed should he not? He is my friend. He knows I am short of grass. Surely the rest follows naturally."

"Too naturally for me," she said. "Art Chesseldine, if you want the truth, is a cattle thief and—"

"Blanca! I will not hear such words. I forbid you—"

"Furthermore," she cut through his talk, "he is the one who tried to take that money away from me—ask this man. He heard them talking."

"What!" cried Don Leo, surging up from his chair. And even Gonzales, the foreman, looked startled.

Bender recrossed his legs. "I can't say about that. I did hear some talk. The big wheel of this bunch was a fellow called 'Art' but—"

The girl said impatiently, "What other Art is there?"

Her father looked shaken. Gonzales, in English, asked, "How well could you see these man?"

"Not very well, though I might recognize his voice." A silence built up and Bender said at last, reluctantly, "I think the girl is right. They knew about the money. They were expecting a man from a ranch and it was plain from their talk they weren't hunting no gringo."

Don Leo, still frowning, abruptly pulled up his head. He looked briefly toward the couch then gave his guest a quizzical smile. "Because my daughter happens to be beautiful does not make her always right. How can I believe that a man who has sat at my table and given every assurance of being my friend—"

"Does a coyote have friends?" Blanca's eyes flashed round scornfully. "Does a lobo turn his back on a calf in a bog hole?"

"Enough!" her father shouted. "Are you the master of Tres Pinos? Am I then become so aged I must seek advice of a woman? *Chihuahua!* A buyer of cattle is not classed as a drifter and a man who has friends who can loan so much money is hardly the kind to become a robber."

"That depends," Bender said, "on things a man don't generally advertise—like the jams he gets into and how bad he needs cash." He considered the next thing he said quite awhile before saying it, finally speaking out anyway. "I understand there's been talk this fellow might be a rustler."

"Mother of God," exclaimed Don Leo, sinking into his chair, "must we credit the rumors given wing by our enemies? Anything can be heard if one stretches the ear enough and my daughter has not cared for this man from the first. She hears these wild stories and, because we lose a few cattle, she declares he has stolen them . . . whereas we will probably discover that our cows have merely strayed."

"Still it's queer," Bender said, "that he should be the one to speak to you about these leases, that he should understand your interest and be so certain you'd need money that in advance of speaking about it he should even arrange for the loan."

Don Leo frowned and tapped the arms of his chair. "I can hardly see a mountain where a molehill fails to exist."

"Well, it's none of my business," Bender shrugged, and Blanca said, "Would you like, papa mio, to hear the rest of our experiences?"

"Carai!" he said. "Is there more?"

"The first shot was mine. When I saw how they had me cut off from Tres Pinos I fired my pistol, hoping you would hear it. They came so fast and all about me I dared not make another sound. No one knew who fired the shot and this one they called Art became very excited. One was sure it was Pete but this man Art had other notions. He said it was a lot of money and that one of the others was trying to get it for himself and go away with it. The other men did not like this. There was a little more talk and then one man said. 'There is a stray down here somewhere,' and I supposed he had seen me. So, when this mysterious Art said each man should move forward and call out his name, I threw my pistol farther into the canyon. It struck a rock loudly and everyone commenced shooting."

Then she told about Bender knocking her horse down, about him picking her up and about his horse being shot out from under them. She really did quite a job, being very dramatic, and when she came to the fight at the cabin even the senora's mouth dropped open and her father said, *"Sangre de Cristo!"* She told of hiding the money, of digging it up again, and claimed the Texan had cut down some seven or eight men before the Tres Pinos cowboys had got there to help them.

"Ha, ha!" laughed Don Leo, abruptly recovering his good spirits. *"Muy hombre!"* he said, grinning, as though this were the best news he'd heard in a long while.

"Shucks," Bender scowled, "I probably didn't kill any of them—leastways not more'n a couple." But the old man wouldn't have him playing it down. It was plain he considered this traveling man from Texas a kind of second Billy the Kid. And there wasn't much doubt but that his foreman did, also. Gonzales did not look happy.

Bender took the occasion to ask the old rancher if he'd known of the man who had made him the loan. "No," smiled Don Leo, "but his *dinero* is 'sta bueno and now we shall bid in those eight thousand acres and have grass *mucho mucho* for all of my cattle."

He had broken into English in his pleasure and excitement but Bender went on following the thought in his head. "You hadn't ever heard of him but still you were sure he would make you the loan?"

"But, of course. My good friend, Senor Chesseldine, had told me he would. Should one contemplate the teeth of a gift horse?"

"Sometimes," said Bender, "that can be a good idea. What's the name of this gent that chucks his dough around so easy? An old settler, is he, or one of these Johnny-Come-Latelys?"

"I think," Blanca said, "he was just there to lend the money."

The old don, with a look of long suffering, ignored her. "His name is Lasham," he answered politely. "Aaron Abijah Lasham."

4 | DELILAH OF THREE PINES

BENDER sat very still and felt the cold stiffness coming over his face. He became aware of Don Leo with his cheeks like fried parchment shrinking back in his chair, and only then did he realize he'd got out of his own. He took his hand off the old man's shoulder and swiveled his head till he could catch the bulging eyes of Pete Gonzales and the distended cigarette-yellowed fingers that were spread above the butt of the gun at his groin. "You saw the guy. Tell me, was he thin or fat? *Speak!*" Bender snarled in the voice of a cougar.

The edges of the foreman's hair gleamed raw red in the lampglow. He had to sponge his lips with his tongue three times before he could get any words out, and even then they were unintelligible.

"Speak out! Was he *fat?*" Bender's eyes blazed like hellfire and the Mexican, making the sign of the Cross, gulped noisily, jerkily nodding. *"Si . . . mucho mas . . .* like the hog," he said, blanching; and Bender cursed in a passion.

"Jesus and Mary!" exclaimed Don Leo, jumping up. "Must you talk in this way before women?"

Bender stared. "You may sound a little mixed up yourself, old man, when you understand whom you've to deal with. This fine friend of your friend is Deef Lasham, the sheep king, and if you can't add that up you'd better go back to school because you sold out the cows when you signed that skunk's paper."

"Sheep!" The old *ranchero* looked stunned. "You think he might bring these sheep into the Potrillos?"

Bender laughed harshly. "I don't *have* to think, damn it! Why do you suppose he loaned you that money?" He did not wait for an answer; he started cursing again. Up and down the great room he strode with his face black as thunder, and no one ventured a word until Blanca, with a shudder, said, "I was right, after all."

"Right?" Bender shouted. "You didn't guess the least half of it! This deal was so slick you're licked no matter what you do. All that guy needs is a foothold, the thinnest kind of excuse—and you've made him a partner in this Tres Pinos Rancho!"

Don Leo pulled his chin off his chest. "That is not so," he said stiffly. "I have given him a lien against the ranch and that is all. When I pay—"

"You'll never get the chance to pay him off," said Bender flatly. "He won't give you any chance—this ain't a game he plays for marbles. He don't handle his sheep like they do in the stories. This guy's *big business!* His crew's as different from the old-time sheepherders as wolves are from rabbits. In the old days the herders walked, like *peones.* Lasham's men don't walk, they ride like *caballeros.* He's got a bunch of Yaqui Indians and feeds them well on other folks' beef. He gives every *pelado* a .30-30 rifle and all he ever tells them is 'Feed my sheep.' What chance have you got against a bunch like that?"

Don Leo reared back his head and glared. "You shall see!"

he said sternly. "Those sheep will not come here—in the country, perhaps, but not on Tres Pinos. My *vaqueros* will see to that, I assure you."

Bender looked at him sadly. "Well, I hope you are right. But there was a guy thought like you do back home in West Texas; he was a plenty tough hombre and he went on the prod. He got together his men and established a deadline. It didn't keep Lasham from getting what he wanted. He warned him: 'Deadlines ain't legal,' but the guy kept his chin out. Then Lasham moved in. He lost a couple of Indians but they put the sheep all over this guy's place. Then the law took this fellow and put a rope around his neck for killing those two herders."

"That will not happen to me," declared the *ranchero* fiercely. "My people have fought *los Indios* for hundreds of years. This ranch is mine and I shall keep it. That man in Texas, if he had enough men, could have kept those sheep away from him. We have no laws around here which cause a man to be hanged for protecting his property. Let them try to bring sheep here—"

"Okey," Bender said, "but they'll do it. You've got two strikes against you already. This Chesseldine's had a good chance to look around. While he was eating at your table you can bet he sized this place up, and you can bet whatever he saw was passed right straight along to Lasham. He'll know exactly how you're fixed, how many men you've got and everything, including the way your land lays. On top of all that he owns a piece of your ranch—"

"What this man says," declared Gonzales in Spanish, "can apply just as well to himself as to another."

"Right as rain," Bender smiled, and got heavily out of his chair and stood up. The look he passed from range boss to owner showed plainly the hardness that had been ground into him by too much experience too swiftly acquired. "I'm just telling you," he said, "the way it stacks up to me."

"What do you think I should do?" asked Don Leo.

Bender shook his head, frowning. "Best thing you can do is dig a hole an' crawl into it. But if I was in your boots," he

grumbled, sliding into English, "I'd make a blue streak gettin'
that mazuma back to Lasham. I don't expect he would take it
even if you could find him because that's probably the edge
he's settin' up his plans on. But if I was you I think I'd try it.
Failin' that, I'd say you better lay in some strychnine because,
whenever he's ready, he's goin' to move in here just as sure
as God builds them little green apples."

Gonzales said, sneering: "Too much you know about these
man."

"Right again, Pedrocito. I know that guy like the back of
my hand."

"Perhaps, papa mio," Blanca said without expression, "you
might persuade Mr. Bender to stay on at Three Pines and sell
you the advantage of his experience in this matter."

Bender's look turned stiff as frostbite. "Not me," he said
curtly—"ain't no use of you askin'. I know when I'm well off."

Gonzales' laugh held an open contempt.

Bender read the same thought in the girl's climbing eyebrows but he'd had all of Deef Lasham that he was aiming
to stomach. Let them think what they wanted. Only a fool
tried to buck a stacked deck and he was all done with being
a fool for Aaron Abijah Lasham.

Don Leo smiled brightly. "The very thing," he said. "A
man of your parts would know how to deal with that one
much better than my people. Every man on the place shall be
at your disposal. Consider it, my friend. With such an army
behind you this man would not dare to bring his sheep on
Tres Pinos—but you are tired," he said contritely. "We will
talk of this in the morning."

"In the morning," Bender said, "I'm gettin' out of this
country."

HE had meant every word of that firm resolution, but he
had not reckoned with Blanca. Don Leo was waiting in the
patio for him when he came out of his room before the sun
had got up. *"Buenos dias, senor.* Our breakfast is waiting. I
hope you find our poor food to your liking."

Not a word about the horse or about leaving, Bender noticed. But if the old man wanted to swap small talk that was all right with him. When he got some hot grub stowed under his belt he was going to get out of here, horse or no horse. So he dragged up a smile and answered politely, following Don Leo into the *comedor*. There, to his disgust, he found Blanca already seated. She looked cool and breezy in a fresh gingham print and greeted his arrival with a very artful smile. "I hope you slept well in our poor bed, Mr. Bender. You weren't too cold, were you?"

"I slept all right," he answered, and slid into a chair without enlarging on the matter. The meal, a very good one, progressed pleasantly enough with the old man talking about conditions in the region, the price of beef and some horses he had seen during the racing at Silver City. He asked if Bender were acquainted with Herefords and, when he said he was, he asked some thoughtful questions about them, telling Bender afterwards he hoped some day to raise them. "I saw a few head last spring at El Paso—magnificent animals! Less stock and better quality would appear to be the answer on a range such as ours."

After the *moza* had fetched their coffee and they'd pushed back their chairs for a comfortable smoke, the old fox got around to what was filling his mind. "With less horns and more beef," he said, "my range, with the land I plan to lease from *los Indios,* will be able very well to accommodate two outfits. On Tres Pinos there are two spring-fed lakes, one of which is near these lease lands."

He must have read Bender's mind about then for, turning, he said abruptly, "My foreman, Pete, will be here in a moment to take you around to have a look at our horses. Should it be your wish to leave I will put nothing in your way; but, first, I have a small matter I should like to put before you."

"If the main thing behind it is to keep me around," Bender said, "I ain't interested."

"Frankly, that is true," the old man admitted. He took hold of his whiskers and chewed on his lip, finally saying, "This visit to Deming . . . you could not put it off?"

Bender gave the girl a hard look and said curtly, "I've already tangled with Lasham once and got myself sheeped plumb out of the cow business. I ain't hankerin' to have my ears pinned back again."

"But this is not Texas. We do things differently here. Tres Pinos is patented land, every acre, and the law gives a rancher the right to protect it. If you will stay here and help me against this *picaro,* I will give you one lake and a whole mile around it, in addition," he said grimly, "to the lease lands for which I have borrowed this money. All this I will give you plus one half of my cattle."

Bender's mouth fell wide open. He pulled it shut with a scowl and blackly stared at the girl, convinced in his own mind that she was behind this. He recalled what she had told him last night about the desert, about the men who came across it, and began to understand then how this kind of deal made sense. *You are not the first Texican who has come up off that desert, but you're cut to the pattern.* That was it, all right. That fight at the shack was the clincher.

But where else would he get such a chance to start over? It was a bonafide offer, Don Leo was dead serious.

He squirmed around in his chair and rasped his jowls with damp fingers. Eight thousand acres of grass and a lake, and half of the Tres Pinos cattle to stock it! A man would be a fool to turn his back on such an offer.

But then he remembered what was back of this philanthropy. Deef Lasham and his sheep and those kill-hungry Yaquis. Lasham's power and crooked influences. And behind these Lasham's marshal. For anyone else it was still a good offer for, as the old man said, this was New Mexico, not Texas. But it was no damn good for Walt Bender—not with that noose hanging over his head.

He stubbed out his smoke and got up, feeling ringy. "You're better off alone," he said, and picked up his hat.

The girl's eyes raked him scornfully. "Are you so frightened of this man that you would throw away a fortune?"

"Reckon that's about the size of it."

Don Leo sighed, not speaking. "What," Blanca said, "do you have to have to go with us?"

"Aren't you forgettin' what you told me last night?—that nothing ever comes off that desert but trouble? You better thank your stars I'm not stayin'."

Don Leo bowed to the inevitable. *"Dispensame, senor.* I will have my foreman bring you a horse."

Bender watched him step into the patio. Getting old, he thought, and hating to show it.

He felt the demand of the girl's eyes, resenting it. Even across the space of this table, not turning his head, he could feel the vibrant magnetism of her.

She got up. "Some kinds of trouble I can handle. I do not think I could handle your Mr. Deef Lasham."

"That's why I'm goin'. I don't think I could, either."

"But if we're willing to chance that?"

He stepped around the table and saw the pulse in her throat beat quick and hard. He saw her eyes dilate but she didn't back off, didn't try to get away from him even when his hand reached out and gripped her shoulder. The sun flung blue lights through the black of her hair and, twisted by his grip, the thin cotton of her dress was pulled tight across her breasts in a fashion that excited and then enraged him.

He let go of her shoulder as though it had burnt him but her eyes didn't change. He didn't step away, either. All the long hungers were fusing inside him, building up something which was stronger than judgment and made a roaring in his head through which he saw her as a magnificent animal— strong, cruel, tawny as a panther. A beautiful savage, primitive, flawless and entirely desirable. She was a strange wild melody that sang through his blood. And he remembered then one other thing she had told him, that a man never got away from anything by running.

It was the truth.

As from a long way off he heard himself saying, "And when do I get these things your father promised?"

He watched the way her red lips pulled away from bright teeth. "When Tres Pinos no longer finds danger in Lasham. Come—we must tell them you have changed your mind."

5 | A MAN OF THE OLD SCHOOL

HE spent the bulk of that day in the saddle, riding over the place with Don Leo for guide, listening to the old man's stories, discovering the more important landmarks and familiarizing himself with the locations of lakes, trails and outside boundaries. On the south and east Three Pines came against the unbroken dun sea of the desert whose bright glare stretched away through the heat waves and dust devils to the Land of Manana and undiscernible Texas. It was plain enough to Bender then that, if the sheep came off the desert, they could only come onto Don Leo's ranch by way of the trail he himself had ridden. There was no other break in the long line of bluffs here dividing the low from the high lands.

At the cabin in the pines Pete had a crew burying horses but, answering the *patron's* questions, the boss of these swarthy shovelers said they had not come across any dead men. Bender had not been expecting them to, for if he'd actually killed any of that bunch last night, their leader would have been a whole lot too smart, if the man was Art Chesseldine, to leave them around to be identified later. Even the brands had been cut off their horses.

Don Leo had mounted him on an exceptionally fine dun with a brown dorsal stripe and zebra markings on the knees. The animal had been gelded, was very handy and quick and showed many signs of having considerable endurance. The *ranchero* rode another which looked amazingly like it and, when Bender complimented him on the quality of these horses, the girl's father said the strain had been in the family many years, having been started by his grandfather, a man of many parts. The family had ranched near Durango in those days and done a little mining on the side when pressed for cash. Bender thought it was too bad they hadn't a mine to fall back on now.

Dusk was thickening fast when they returned that evening and two peons came running to care for their horses. Bender said he would see to his own, would then eat with the crew and sleep in the bunkhouse, but the old man would not hear of it. "No, *amigo,* you have a room already and a man in your position—"

"Yeah," Bender nodded, "suppose you tell me about that. If I'm to work with your crew won't they think it damn funny if I'm put up in the house?"

"You will not work with the crew—that is my foreman's concern. You are officially my guest and will so continue until I shall be rid of this accursed sheepman."

Bender had to admit that this would cause less friction though he didn't like the thought of being so much around Blanca. She was a deal too disturbing; and then, besides, there was Gonzales. Unless he'd misread completely the signs observed last night, the foreman was not going to like having them share adjoining rooms.

He'd been somewhat puzzled himself when he had first discovered they were doing so, for this seemed to him to be contrary to much that he had heard of Spanish-American customs, which were mostly rather astringent as regarded unmarried young women. Now, more familiar with the layout, he could see they had not had any great choice, the only other available room being the much larger one shared by her father and mother which they probably considered too near to the bunkhouse. Not that the breaking of any stuffy convention was likely to bother overmuch a girl as forthright as Blanca.

So, though he was far from being pleased with the arrangement, he said nothing more but, picking up Chucho's reins, led the horse around back and through the high gate which gave onto the *parada,* as the open ground was called between the stables and the quarters given over to the men. After caring for the horse and making sure he was properly fastened in for the night, Bender was about to head for the passage leading into the patio when he observed two shapes against the bunkhouse wall. Both men were watching him and one of them was Gonzales.

Three hanging lanterns had been lighted to illuminate the *parada* and, although it was still pretty much filled with shadows, he could see well enough not to care for the expression on the foreman's face.

As he was about to move along Gonzales stepped from the wall. "Hold on," he said in Spanish, and the other lounged forward and barred Bender's way.

"Well," Bender said, "what's on your mind, Pedrocito?"

"I want to know why you are staying here."

"Why don't you ask the *patron* if you're curious?"

"I'm asking you, Gringo."

Both men were armed and Gonzales looked ugly. The second man was heavier with a hairline that came almost down to his eyebrows, a burly ruffian with mismatched eyes and the mark of a knife across one cheekbone.

Bender, caught off balance and at the decided disadvantage of not wanting trouble in a place of their choosing, tried to swallow his outrage and said, thinking fast, "I am staying because I've been asked to stay. The *patron*—"

"Do not lie to me, Gringo"

"Why would I be lying? You heard the talk last night. You must have heard Don Leo—"

"He but agreed with his daughter. He did not ask you to stay—"

"He asked me this morning. At breakfast."

Gonzales stared at him, scowling. "I think you make this up. Even if it should be as you say about this sheepman, why would a gringo put himself out for a Mexican man old enough to be—"

"Well, you've got something there," Bender grumbled. "As a matter of fact, he made me a proposition. Because of what happened at that shack on the bluffs your boss has me pegged for a second Bill Bonney. He said, if I will stay and buck

Lasham and keep the sheep out of here he will make me a present of those lease lands, the upper lake and half of his cattle."

"What!" cried Gonzales. "Do you think I am a *fool?*"

With his face contorted by a terrible anger he caught the Texan's arm in a grip of steel and, before Bender quite realized what was happening, the scar-faced man had pulled open the *parada* gate and he was being shoved through. "There—" snarled Gonzales, pointing, "there is the road. Now go!"

Before Bender could speak there was a commotion behind them and a roar from Don Leo that made both men jump. "What is this?"

He flung Scar Face aside with the flap of a hand, catching Pedro's shirt at the throat with the other and slamming his shoulders hard against the adobe wall.

"Is a guest to be turned from my house like a beggar? *Sangre de Christo!* Ungrateful son of a goat! What is this you would do behind my back? *Habla! Pronto!*"

Gonzales quailed from his glare. His *compadre* took this chance to slink away in the shadows.

Don Leo shook Gonzales until the man's mouth fell open. *"Andale—habla!* What is this you would do, eh?"

The foreman caught up with his breath. "This man said—"

"And who are you to question the remarks of a guest? Since when have you become the master of Tres Pinos? Tell me that!"

"It was for your own good entirely. This *gringo* comes here with his lies and you swallow them—"

With a curse Don Leo struck Gonzales across the face. "Begone, ungrateful dog! Get back to your kennel. I will deal with you later."

AFTER supper, when he was walking with the *ranchero* in the patio, Bender said out of a thoughtful silence, "Don't believe I'd say any more to your foreman. He had your interests—"

"This is good of you, my friend." Don Leo stopped beside the fountain. "A forgiving spirit reflects much credit, but . . ."

He spread his hands with a shrug. "Let us talk of something better."

There was a barrel standing handy about two feet this side of the shrubbery and Bender, about to settle his hip, was astonished when the rancher plucked him unceremoniously away from it. *"Dispensame, senor,* but there is an unpleasant death in that barrel. A coral snake, you understand, that was trapped near the fountain by one of my *mozos."*

Bender, startled, thumbed a match to flame and saw the sinuous shape transversely banded in red, yellow and black, the lightning-swift flick of its darting red tongue, the black snout with its horrible eyes staring up at him; and he drew back, his flesh creeping. "You ought to kill that damn thing!"

"I have a friend at Santa Rosa who will be very pleased to get hold of that fellow. He is making a collection of poisonous reptiles."

"And he'll collect a quick grave if that bastard gets hold of him." Bender tossed the burnt matchstick into the fountain. "I'm pulling out in the morning."

Don Leo's face turned sober. He put a hand on Bender's shoulder. "I beg of you, *amigo,* do not say that you are leaving. Ask what you will but do not tell me that."

"All I could bring you by remaining is trouble. This business of Gonzales has shown me the truth—you'd be playing right into the sheep crowd's hands. If you're going to buck Lasham you don't want no man of straw."

"Straw man—you?" The old *ranchero* laughed. "You make joke . . . ees too fonny." Then he said, swinging back into Spanish again, "Stay, my friend. I will flog that dog of a Pedro. I will . . . eh?"

"Would you place a rotten apple in the crate with the good ones?" Bender's hard unhumorous smile crossed his lips. He cuffed the dust from his hat against the side of a leg. "You can't fight Lasham with gallows bait, pardner. Across the line, back in Texas, I'm wanted for murder."

"Carai! What is this?" Don Leo exclaimed, but he did not look in the least disconcerted. "In the heat of passion a man does many things he will spend the rest of his life regretting.

This I understand; but do not ask me to believe you'd kill a man without good reason."

"I didn't kill him," said Bender harshly, "but one day the law will catch up with me. And if it catches me here you'll be done for."

"Have no fear about that. My little Blanca has told me how you stood off those *ladrones;* how you saved her life and—what is more precious—her virtue from those *bandidos.* Do I forget that? Never! So be of good cheer. If you did not kill the man perhaps we can prove—"

"Not a chance," Bender growled. "It was Lasham who framed me because he wanted my grass. The fellow who was killed was a Texas state senator who was ready to put the skids under Lasham, but no one will believe that because he worked for the Pool. I can see it all now . . . why they kept shoving me this way . . . Lasham's aiming to use me to get his hooks on Tres Pinos."

"He will not get Tres Pinos!"

Don Leo rose from his chair and commenced pacing the grass, chin bowed in thought until at last, wheeling round, he snarled, "A curse on this man, this *hijo de diablo!* We are not beaten yet and, if you stay, we shall not be." He struck his fist into his hand and glared at Bender fiercely. "My people are fighters with much experience of *Indios;* they will not run away from this *Tejanno* and his *Yaquis.* You will find, my friend, that this is different than Texas. Here the laws will protect the cattle—"

Bender shook his head, sighing. "That's what they said in Grand Falls, too, until Lasham's fine friends and the sheep pool made new ones."

"No matter! They will not make new ones here, I can tell you. The Spanish Americans run the government here and they have no love for these *Texanos.* No, my friend, you have given me your word and I shall hold you to it. Here you shall stay till we are rid of this devil!"

"Well . . . if you feel that way about it, all right," Bender frowned, "but don't say I didn't warn you. Now, what about this Texican sheriff you've got—this Cash Fentress?"

Don Leo brushed Fentress aside with a smile. "If that one should get too big for his saddle, we shall call in my good friend Don Ramon Eusebio de Vega at Santa Fe. And tomorrow you shall go and make the bid on those lease lands. So be of good heart; we will show these dogs of *Texanos* that Spanish Americans know how to fight for their grass."

6 | AND NOW IT BEGINS

WITH his big-roweled spurs clawing sound from the board walk, Bender strode by the side of Pedro Gonzales who had not said one word since they had quitted the ranch. They'd got off to a good early start before daylight and, though it yet lacked three hours before the bids would be opened, already the town appeared crammed full to bursting. The street was a clutter of spring wagons and buckboards and hitched horses made an almost solid line at the tie racks.

Quite a place, this Deming; a lot larger than he'd imagined. It might be a railroad town like he'd heard, for there were the gleaming iron rails over yonder, but this morning the cow crowd had taken it over. Big hats and boots were the order of the day and everywhere men cried out greeting to Gonzales so that they were continually stopping while he swapped comments and badinage with people of his acquaintance. More than one of these *vaqueros* sent covert glances at Walt Bender, surprised no doubt to see their friend strolling cheek by jowl with a gringo. It must have graveled Gonzales plenty, yet not by a word or the edge of a look did the Three Pines foreman admit Bender existed.

Which was all right with Bender. He had enough on his mind without having to keep up with any double-faced talk. Somewhere in this mob of milling gun-hung riders there would be, he felt certain, at least one man representing Deef Lasham, and his interest at the moment centered in picking that one out. For it did not make sense that Lasham ever had intended to let any other bunch get hold of grass he wanted.

The bidding on these Indian lands was scheduled to take place in one of the railroad warehouses just across the tracks, and he found it no job at all to tell which one by the size of the crowd hanging round in front. The long plank platform already was thronged with jostling shapes in all manner of clothing and the street before it showed a lot of the over-flow standing round in gesticulating groups, some talking vociferously, all boisterous, many laughing—all in a holiday mood by the look of them.

The biggest part of the crowds were solidly Mexican, the fat and portly Dons extremely gay in their colorful finery, their swaggering cigarette-smoking foremen looking very impor-tant with their groups of *vaqueros,* the only sour notes to be seen anywhere being made by the gringos.

It was these Bender paid most attention to. He didn't see any of them laughing. They stood apart by themselves in little knots of twos and threes looking surly and suspicious with their bleak, bony faces and hard-eyed stares. He did see three or four who looked both well fed and pompous, and his lips curled with scorn. They reminded him of Toby Bronsen and were obviously politicians.

Gonzales presently touched his sleeve, breaking abruptly his long front of silence. "We are going to eat. Over there," he pointed.

"Suits me," Bender nodded. "I could use some grub myself."

Dislike was a plain and undisguised scowl on the face of Don Leo's segundo. Outrage made his green eyes look like emeralds, but he swung away without answering, Bender fol-lowing. When Gonzales sat down with his friends at a table Bender sat with them, not caring what they thought, caring less that they ignored him. He knew Deef Lasham's methods. Someone at Tres Pinos, he would have bet his last centavo, was in the sheepman's pay, and he did not propose to let Pedro get out of his sight for a moment.

THE auctioneer took his stand at one o'clock. He was a
deputy commissioner and one of the politicians Bender previ-
ously had noticed, a burly blowsy-faced man in a top hat and
tailcoat. "This federal auction," he intoned, "is to place by
public bidding certain lands in the care of the Indian Department . . ."

He got through his preamble in less than two minutes, then
explained how the land had been thrown into blocks, specify-
ing by acres how much each contained; Block 10, much the
smallest, was the one Tres Pinos wanted. "Now we'll open
these bids at ten cents an acre and we'll start with Block 1—"

"Fifteen cents," called a Don in silver-braided sombrero.

"Seventeen!" cried another; and Block 1 was knocked down
at nineteen to the first man when nobody else offered to go
higher.

While the deputy commissioner was going through his legal
description of Block 2, Bender took the opportunity to discover who stood round him, nowhere seeing any member of
Lasham's crowd he was able to recognize. When the second
block was bid in at twenty by the same man, Bender's narrow-
ing stare looked him over with a closer interest. He gave his
name as Esteban and was a short, rotund, very haughty looking
hombre whose garb, although expensive, showed a considerable amount of wear about the seat and elbows. When he
also acquired Block 3 at thirty-two Bender nudged Don Leo's
foreman. "Who is this guy?" he asked under his breath.

Gonzales shrugged. "He is a small *ranchero* from the vi-
cinity of Holy Cross."

"Holy Cross, eh? What's he want with all that land away
to hell an' gone away from him?"

Gonzales shrugged. He turned around and became engrossed in a conversation with a man on the other side of him.
When he again faced front he said without inflexion, "This
man thinks Don Esteban is buying for some people who
haven't appeared here."

This coincided with Bender's thought and, when the fellow
bid in Block 4 at forty, Bender said to the deputy commissioner, "I understand these bids are in U. S. dollars."

"That's correct."

"Cash on the barrelhead?"

"Naturally the money must be put in my hands before these lands are disposed of—"

"Before this shindig is over?"

"Yes, of course—"

"I ain't seen you take any of that fellow's dough yet."

The deputy commissioner wiped his face with a handkerchief. A jabber of talk started up all around him while he peered at Bender with an irritable frown. "I can't see what difference that makes to you," he said at last. "I haven't heard anyone else here objecting and you're not making any bids that I've noticed—"

"I'll bid," Bender said, "when I want to buy something."

"Then what're you butting in now for?"

"I'm hankerin' to see the color of that guy's money."

There were half a dozen others who seemed to have the same feeling, and now these all commenced talking at once. The deputy commissioner got red in the face and banged with his gavel till he got enough quiet to make himself heard. But, before he could get his voice into action, a bleach-eyed cowman to the left of him cried: "B'Gawd, he's right—let's see this bird pay fer what he's got already!"

Don Esteban scornfully waddled over to the clerk, whipped out a well stuffed money belt and counted the purchase price into his hands. It came to slightly in excess of one hundred thousand dollars and many of those nearest, seeing that none of this currency was beneath a four-numbers figure shook their heads in awe. But when the corpulent Don, jamming the receipts in his pocket, got back to where he'd been doing his bidding, Bender saw him mutter to a tall beak-nosed Mexican who'd been standing beside him and, a little bit later, saw that man leave the building.

Bender bided his time and, when Esteban opened the next block at twenty, he said, "I'll bid fifty."

The fat Mexican glared. He finally said, "Fifty-five."

"Seventy," Bender said, and there was a sharp startled silence.

The deputy commissioner mopped off his face again. "You aim to let that bid stand?"

"Thought I told you I'd bid when I—"

"Eighty!" snarled Don Esteban.

The stillness grew brittle.

The deputy commissioner looked nervously at Bender. "Well!" he said, scowling. "You goin' to bid any more?"

"Not on that chunk. He's gone too high for me."

There were several cries of *"Ladron!"* and hard looks and grumbling all around the deputy commissioner; and several of the Mexicans who had come there to bid, but didn't have that kind of money, wheeled about in their tracks and, cursing, departed. One glowering Texan in a shirt stained with sweat told the clerk in a snarl to hurry up and take his money. "Some of us boys has got better things t' do than hang an' rattle in this bake oven watchin' that greaser lord it over white men."

Bender halfway looked for some of the other Dons to take umbrage, and he did see a couple of them drop their hands to knife hilts, but the most of the Spanish Americans on tap appeared too incensed with the man themselves to much care what a damned gringo called him.

Several of them crowded around to watch him count out the money, their own lips moving in unison as bill after bill fluttered down on the table. Block 5 had cost Esteban twenty thousand dollars.

It was while the legal description of Block 6 was being read that Bender became aware of Pete Gonzales' startled interest. The man was watching him like a hawk, the ugly suspicions churning back of his eyes telling all too plainly what direction his thoughts were taking.

"Don't let the tail wag the dog," Bender told him and, to the man with the gavel, "If you're ready on Block 6 I'll give forty cents an acre."

"Forty-five," grumbled Esteban.

"Forty-eight," said the Texan in the dusty, sweat-stained shirt.

Esteban growled without turning, "Fifty."

"Sixty-five," Bender muttered, and Esteban stared at him blackly.

"Seventy!"

Bender fished out the makings and twisted up a smoke. "Fifty-seven thousand acres," he told the deputy commissioner reflectively, "at seventy cents an acre comes to thirty-nine thousand, nine hundred dollars. Quite a parcel of money. Do you reckon he's got it?"

The government man looked at Esteban. The Mexican swore in three different dialects. Bender said, "I think you better make sure," and moved up to the table to see for himself.

Esteban jerked out his poke in a rage and commenced counting. He piled thirty-nine thousand dollar bills on the table and was beginning to sweat when Beak-Nose pushed up through the crowd with the rest of it.

Bender grinned sourly. "Okay. Let him have it."

HE went back and beckoned Gonzales to the door and stepped outside with him. "I've got five hundred smackers," he said without preamble. "That's Lasham's dough that's biddin' in these leases and I been tryin' to make the bastard whittle it down where he can't hurt us. But you saw that guy come in just then; he's fetched him another roll and now I don't know whether we'll cut it or not. When Don Leo gave you the money to bid with this mornin' did he give you anything over that forty-five hundred?"

Gonzales shook his head. He began to look worried.

"Well, there's nothin' we can do about it," Bender said, "but hope for the best. That roll he just got looked big enough to choke a horse, but it's handled dough that's been in circulation. There might not be any grand notes in it. If I can just make that clown bid enough on these next three. . . ." He let the rest trail off and they went back inside.

Block 7 had been bid in while they'd been talking outside. It had gone at forty-five to the sweaty-shirted Texan who was now counting his money onto the table in front of the clerk. There was a look of satisfaction on his harsh wind-roughened countenance as, folding the clerk's receipt, he buttoned it into his shirt's left pocket. With a short ugly laugh he shouldered Esteban out of his way, saying as he strode past Bender, "There's *one* that range-hoggin' spik didn't git!"

Bender grunted, not at all sure he liked the sudden turn this thing had taken. He opened Block 8 with a bid of twenty cents.

Encouraged by the Texican's experience a dark slender man with bells on his sombrero hesitantly called, "Twenty-five," and the crowd looked at Esteban. The portly Mexican stared back at them, his gashlike mouth tightly folded across his teeth.

The deputy commissioner looked at him unhappily, finally mopping his cheeks with the limp piece of rag that still dangled bedraggled from his pudgy left fist. "You care to bid on this block, Mister Esteban?"

"No!"

One of the hard-faced crew against the back wall said, "Twenty-six."

The man with the bells said, "Twenty-eight," and got it.

Bender saw the play now clearly. This was no spur-of-the-moment affair but a plan that had been gone over and over, a plan engineered with all someone's cunning. The pool never had intended to bid in *all* of these lease lands; the farthermost grass was what they had been after to cloak their stealing of the rest with an appearance of legality. Bender had bothered them in only one particular, forcing their agent to pay more than had been counted on. The new roll just now hurried in by Hook Nose was brought to secure Block 10, the grasslands bordering the north of Don Leo's holdings.

Lasham, to get his sheep onto pasture in the grass he'd got already, was going to have to cross Tres Pinos or go five hundred miles out of his way. No court in the land would expect a man to make a swing of that magnitude; and the lien he had on Tres Pinos would go a long way toward establishing his right to cross it. Now, if, in addition he got hold of Block 10 he would have any court fight licked before it started.

Tres Pinos had one chance left as Bender saw it. And this had to hinge on how badly he'd strained their available cash by running the cost of those earlier blocks up. They knew how much money Don Leo had but they may not have counted on aid coming from Bender. This, then, was their chance, the only one Walt could see.

For the pool wasn't dumb like this nump they had bidding; the moment they'd got word from Esteban's messenger they'd have known Bender'd run the cost up on a bluff.

BLOCK 9 went the way of the last two, with Esteban never even opening his mouth.

The stillness in this room became increasingly more intense as the deputy commissioner bucked his way through the abstracts of legal phraseology, preparatory to the throwing open of Block 10 for bidding. Whether anyone here—aside from Walt, Gonzales and, possibly, Esteban—fully understood Don Leo's situation, or had heard of the note he had given to raise money, more than a few must have realized his pressing need for additional range and sensed in this parcel a partial answer to his problems. This was implicit in the looks now flashed at his foreman.

A fine sweat broke out upon Gonzales' florid cheeks. He scrinched green eyes against the smoke from his cigarette and straightened bony shoulders.

A man across the room opened the bidding at fourteen cents. Another called "Fifteen"—Esteban raising it two. The original bidder went up one more cent and Gonzales then said twenty.

With a scornful sneer Esteban made it thirty and Gonzales hiked it another ten.

Grinning maliciously, Esteban said, "Fifty-five," like that settled it, and commenced pushing his way toward the clerk's writing table.

The man representing the Indian Department took a long hard look at Gonzales and let his breath out. He allowed his glance, through the smoke haze, to rummage a few other faces. "Fifty-five cents on eight thousand acres is forty-four hundred dollars. If there are no further bids on this parcel—"

"Fifty-six," Bender said.

It couldn't have caused more commotion if he had hauled out his sixgun. The commissioner's mouth dropped open. The clerk closed his eyes. Esteban whirled from the table with a bleating screak of outrage.

The deputy commissioner mopped his face and looked unduly perturbed.

"Is—is that a legitimate bid?"

Bender nodded.

The man from the Indian Department sent a fluttery look at Lasham's livid agent, who snatched up his money with a furious oath.

"How can these man do these thing?"

"Chew or spit," Bender said. "Do you want it?"

Esteban's face turned an unhealthy gray. He put a tongue across his lips. He finally groaned "Fifty-seven," and you could just about hear him.

Bender said, stony faced, "Sixty-two," and watched the fat Mexican stagger into the crowd.

Someone let out a yell and the three or four Texicans still in the building began whooping and pummeling each other's backs. The deputy commissioner banged with his gavel and a ripple of motion ran through a group round the doorway. "If there are no further bids, Block 10 goes to—What'd you say your name was?"

"Name's Bender, but—"

And that was where the breath got suddenly hung in Bender's throat.

A pair of men were shoving toward him, the crowd falling back around them. Both had leveled guns in their hands. Something winked coldly from the second man's shirt, but it was the first who caught and held Bender's stare.

The man had on a red hat. He was short, broad and burly, with a weather-blackened skin and a heavy cropped mustache that did not even begin to hide the arrogant curl of his gun fighter's lips. This was Syd Hazel, boss of Lasham's sheep.

He indicated Bender with a jerk of his gun snout. "There's

your turkey, Fentress. I'll arrange for extradition. You won't have no trouble collectin' the bounty."

The deputy commissioner peered around as in a daze, finally appealing bewilderedly to obvious authority. "What's—"

"Disregard that last bid," Hazel snapped at him. "This fellow's a criminal wanted for murder. As such, not entitled to bid on anything."

7 | DARK PURPOSE

BENDER sat on the jail cot's lumpy mattress and tried to think what chance he'd had for handling this different. He may have had such a chance but he was damned if he could find it. The one essential factor which had never entered his head was that Lasham could become so uncontrollably enraged that he would sacrifice everything, every plan he had laid, by sending out the order for his scapegoat's arrest.

For that was Bender's role, all right. From the very start, in the sheep king's plans, he'd been carefully built up and cleverly made over to serve as whipping boy for Deef Lasham's crimes. Every angle, every sequence—those long months of ducking and dodging, gave incontrovertible proof of this truth. There could be no other answer. Lasham's pet marshal had never attempted to come up with him; he'd been satisfied to loaf behind tacking up his damn dodgers.

And here was the essence of the sheep king's craft. Lasham had not wanted Bender caught—you couldn't escape it. Those hand bills had been printed and hung up to keep him moving, to fetch him on the scene of Lasham's next intended project at precisely the time when his arrival could be counted on to more confuse the issue and to strengthen Lasham's hand.

What other interpretation could be put upon the business?

The sheep king considered all cowmen fools and was totally contemptuous of Mexicans. So he would hardly have taken such pains with Bender just to wreck or steal Tres Pinos, even considering its strategic location. These must be the facets of a much larger purpose.

What *was* the man after? Bender asked himself.

He got up and stared out of the narrow barred window, eyes morosely prowling the unlovely view of rusted cans and broken bottles—by-products of the hash house on the one side and of the honkytonk on the other. Beyond these mounds of discarded trash the range ran bleak and brown to the footslopes of the Florida Mountains.

He gripped the bars with his hands and stared unseeingly between them for long uncounted moments while his still incredulous mind refused to believe Deef Lasham was done with him. It didn't anyplace make sense, which was one of the reasons they had taken him without gunplay when they'd come barging into that warehouse. It was much easier to think that Syd Hazel, without sufficient knowledge of his overlord's final objectives, had acted on his own in bringing off this coup.

For it had been a coup—there was no getting around that. With one quick swoop Lasham's gun boss had put Bender completely out of commission, grabbed the land he'd taken away from them and killed Three Pines' last hope of wriggling clear.

Bender, conceding these facts, remained dissatisfied. He was wholly unable to convince himself these were the ends for which Lasham had groomed him. Had he finished what he'd been going to say, that he'd bid in Block 10 for Tres Pinos, he would have understood this better, for then it might have been argued he had achieved the sheep king's intentions. But he hadn't had time to give more than his name; there'd been no public connection between himself and Don Leo.

The sun must have dropped behind Red Mountain. Mile-long shadows lay across the range, thickening fast in the gathering dusk. The Floridas, southeast, were all blues and purples; and Bender turned from the window thinking briefly of Blanca. He need not ask what she'd say when she heard of the outcome. A tenuous hope which had failed of its purpose, she would write him off as a casualty to the sheep crowd and cast about her for some better weapon.

He moved over to the door and idly scowled through the grating. The corridor was gray with the approach of night and no place in the building could he hear anything stirring. The muted clatter of kettles and hardware and crockery from the hash house next door stirred a faint core of hunger that had been growing in his belly.

He shook the bars and called: "Fentress!" but all he got for an answer were the echoes of his voice.

Shut up and gone off to celebrate, he reckoned; and wondered what would happen to the five hundred dollars the sheriff had taken from his pockets and chucked in the drawer along with his pistol. Not, he decided, that it would make much difference. Money right now was the least of his worries.

He went back and dropped down on the edge of his cot. In another couple hours Gonzales would get back and they would learn at Tres Pinos what had happened to their gun man. He could imagine the yarn the Three Pines ramrod would spin, the importance he would attach to Bender's tame surrender.

But he wasted no futile thoughts about that. What he wanted right now was to get the hell out of here; and he commenced looking round for something he could use.

He didn't find anything. There was the cot and the seatless flush toilet, and alongside the latter there was a damned filthy lavatory that didn't look to have been wiped off since the day it had been installed. The cot was made of iron and had been bolted to the floor. One of those bars covering the window would have made a good weapon, but they were set in solid and he couldn't budge a one of them.

So much for that.

He went back and sat down. He was not resigned to staying here but for the moment, at least, it looked as though he would have to. He stretched out on the lumpy mattress and tried to dream up some way by which he could get the best of whoever came in with his food. He thought of feigning sleep, of pretending to be sick; but when his jailor came at nine he hadn't hit on anything which even remotely looked like being of any use.

He heard the front door bang and then heard bootsteps in the corridor. "I've fetched you some grub," this unseen party said; and there followed a small racket as of a tray being placed on the floor.

"Have I got to eat it in the dark?" Bender growled.

"No. I been fishin' for a match but it looks like I ain't got any. You wait right there. I'll be back in a couple of minutes."

Bootsteps went off down the corridor again. The front door slammed and Bender dropped back on his cot, wondering if all jailors were as absent-minded as this one. Some old man, like as not, which the county was getting for little or nothing.

Still, it seemed a bit odd the sheriff would go off with so small a concern for the safety of his prisoner. He had not impressed Bender as the kind to let a fast buck slip away, and the five hundred dollars collectible in bounty looked a rather substantial nest egg for any such careless handling.

No jail was any stronger than the personnel in charge of keys. Even a fool should be bright enough to figure a man jailed for murder wasn't going to pass up any chances. It was possible, of course, that Fentress had made arrangements which were not yet apparent. And it was possible, too, that such an arrangement was under way. A lot depended, Bender realized, on whether or not the sheep crowd was done with him. If they were, the intention might very well be to engineer an escape which would put Walt Bender where the sheriff could blast him down without danger of repercussions.

The more he thought about that the more he was inclined to believe it was the answer. As things stood right now neither Three Pines nor its owner had been smeared by contact with Bender. If Lasham or Syd Hazel could make it appear that a notorious killer had been loosed by Tres Pinos. . . .

But how the hell could they when Bender, so far as the general public knew, had utterly no connection with Don Leo or his outfit? Was Hazel willing to take the gamble that Bender had been seen enough with Gonzales to establish a connection?

He shook his head, more puzzled than ever. It was not Lasham's style to let any plan go off half cocked. He liked to tie a package up neatly in fancy paper and pretty pink ribbons. Of course they might be in possession of information withheld from Bender which would make a jail break plausible, but he couldn't imagine what that would be.

Turned abruptly motionless, he crouched there, listening, thinking to have caught some furtive sound up yonder; but, if he had, it wasn't repeated, and his mind switched again to the problem he'd shelved earlier. Even in view of his more recent conjecture it still didn't make good sense, to his thinking, that Lasham would have gone to so much bother and now discard him with so little gain to show for it.

There was gain, all right, but it lacked considerable of being anywhere near proportionate to the amount of time and effort which had been expended on saddling Bender with a hired killer's rep.

Turned completely still he probed the corridor's blackness, convinced this time that he had caught a muffled cry. At once, upon its heels, he heard the thud of something falling, the scrape of something dragged. There was someone in the office.

It was the building's total lack of light which really put his teeth on edge. Whatever was being done out there was intended to be kept secret—any nump could figure that. But the question was—from whom?

There came a tiny metallic clatter and again booted feet moved toward him. He said through the blackness: "Find your matches?" The boots came nearer but he didn't get any answer.

Bender's throat began to get dry. After all, he *could* be dry-gulched right here.

The dark silence suddenly exploded in a terrific tinpanny clatter as one of those approaching booted feet whammed into the tray holding Bender's supper. He caught the jolt of a staggering body, a smothered imprecation; and then a girl's scared voice cried tight and frantic: "Bender! Walt! Where are you?"

8 "YOU'RE NOT RUNNING OUT!"

BLANCA!

Relief made the hinges of Bender's knees go wabbly but he got hold of himself, knowing well how little time they might have before somebody stuck his nose into this.

"Here," he called softly, shaking the door's grating. "How'd you manage to get here so quick? Did Gonzales—"

"I haven't seen Pete. I was with that bunch of *peones* on the platform when Fentress brought you out of the warehouse. I came as quick as I dared; I had to locate your horse—"

"Was that you out front? What'd you do with the jailor?"

"I hit him," she said with despair in her voice. "I hid back of the door and when he came in I tripped him. I got his gun away and—"

"All right," Bender said, his words sharp with impatience. "Hurry up and get this door open—"

"I can not find the *keys!*"

She must have caught the sound of his indrawn breath. She moved away from him a little. "I dropped them when that horrible clatter—" Frustration clawed through her desperate tone. He could hear her hands scrabbling round through the dark.

"We've got to work fast," he said. "Strike a light."

"I have no matches."

He listened to her knees thumping round on the floor, the slither and scrape of her searching fingers. Trap smell threatened to cut his breath off. Fright sunk its hooks deep into him and like a man gone berserk he flung his full weight against the steel of the grating. It did no good, of course—none whatever; but he saw now where what had happened here made sense. This girl was the segment which completed the circle. She furnished all they needed to hook him up with Tres Pinos.

She gave a sudden choked cry. He heard her scrambling upright. The blessed clatter of steel against steel as she turned the found key in the lock left him trembling. He felt the grating swing away and then a mutter of voices pulled the slack from his muscles.

"Quick." He caught her arm. He hurried her down the black corridor and into the sheriff's almost-as-black office. "Get the old man's gun—"

"I have it."

"Then get out on the street and walk toward the horses. Whatever you do, *don't run.*"

She pulled open the door. Light from outside turned the gloom a vague gray. His hands found the desk. He heard her move down the steps. He yanked the drawer halfway out and got his gun, got his money. Fiddle scrape and hilarious voices came from the honkytonk to drown any sounds he might otherwise have heard. He thrust the bills in his pocket, the gun in his holster. Its weight did not give him the ease he'd expected. He thought: *Steady does it,* and moved through the door.

Across the way four still shapes were blackly limned against lampglow. The honkytonk fiddles sawed themselves into silence and in the midst of the clapping he pulled the door shut, moving his lips as though talking to someone. Though every sinew cringed he turned around then and tramped down the steps.

The four across the street continued silently to stand there, too far removed for him to make out their faces in that pattern of light and shadow. A rider was coming around the hash house with a led horse; he knew at once that this was Blanca and sensed the sudden interest of the motionless quartet.

If they spoke it was too low for him to hear but he could
tell that they were watching by the stiffness of their postures,
and again fear touched him. Seventy feet of space lay between
himself and them but a .45 could kill at almost double that
distance.

Sweat came out and lay cold against his neck but there
was no help for it. He could not wave the girl back now. He
could turn and move away from her but this he dared not do.

Unaccountably she stopped. He felt his muscles loosen;
then she raised a hand and beckoned.

One of the four across the street half wheeled away from
his companions. Bender did not wait to see what else the
man might do. He was gathering himself to break into a run
when the girl's voice called clearly: "Where will I find the
sheriff?"

Bender felt a little giddy but his mind worked swift as
hers. He threw a hand out. "There's his office but you won't
find him there. I been waitin' half an hour. Nobody there but
the old man and some feller they got in the cooler."

If those men across the street had any connection with
Red Hat or Fentress he did not think this would fool them
very long. But the girl was closer to him than they were and
if he could keep them undecided just a few seconds longer. . . .

He walked toward the girl. "Anything I can do, ma'am?"

"It's about my brother. I was supposed—"

Another dance got started in the honkytonk. "I can't hear
you," Bender shouted, and moved forward as an impatient
man might have done. Of Blanca's reply all he caught was the
one word *jail,* but a look flung over his shoulder disclosed
the gist of it promptly. There were only three shapes on the far
walk now; the other was mounting the sheriff's steps.

Bender let go of caution and broke into a run. A shout
went up behind him. A gun kicked a hole through *Sally
Gooden* and Bender, catching the reins of the led horse,
vaulted into the saddle and they were off in a rush that was
laced with screaming lead.

Bender kneed Chucho right, forcing the girl's horse to whirl
and duck between two buildings. "Go ahead," he growled,

"take the lead an' let's get rollin'. We've got to hit brush before that moon comes up."

She swung her horse ahead and he followed her up an alley and then between two more houses and onto another road and up it hellity larrup. They were heading west and, although he knew Tres Pinos lay somewhere to the south and east, he offered no objections. He glanced back from time to time but the night was too dark for him to make out anything against the lights of the town and the flogging rhythm of the horses' hoofs was too close and too loud for him to hear anything else.

Five minutes later the road forked ahead of them, the left branch turning south, but the girl ignored this and kept on straight ahead across a series of sand drifts and rode another ten minutes before pulling up. They both swung round in their saddles to listen. Then Bender got down and put an ear to the ground.

He climbed back on Chucho and shook his head. "Not a sign. We better cut south now and work around those damn mountains."

"Too long," Blanca answered. "We'll go through them."

BENDER felt none of the elation this escape should have given him. He was alone in the night with a beautiful woman and that didn't cut any ice with him either. He rode with grim face and an increasing feeling of bitter dissatisfaction. He was free for the moment and that was all. Things hadn't changed. This trip had not helped Don Leo. Lasham had got the land he'd been after even though he'd been forced to pay more than intended. Tres Pinos had gotten nothing and Syd Hazel's play, whatever its ultimate intention, made Bender realize very clearly that Lasham wasn't through with him. He'd got away from that jail too easily to be fooled into thinking Lasham's range boss had been caught napping.

After half an hour of riding he put a hand out and pulled up.

"No use in me goin' back there with you."

She pulled in a sharp breath and stared at him. "What do you suppose I got you out of there for?"

"I don't have to guess about that. But it's no good, I tell you. I'm no good to your father now. I've been exposed to your sheriff as a man wanted for murder—"

"If you're afraid," she began, but he cut her off curtly.

"What I'm tryin' to get through your head," he said, "is that all Tres Pinos means to Deef Lasham is a means to an end. As a piece of property he don't give two hoots in hell about your spread. The thing he's after is that two hundred thousand acres of Indian grass!"

She stared at him a moment. He caught the swell of her breasts. "Are you trying to tell me he isn't after our ranch?"

"Sure he's after it; but it's the situation, not the place, he wants. What you've got is a natural gateway, the closest one in reach. So he'll use it. He'll go through it—"

"If he can. That's what I got you out of there for. To stop him."

"I didn't think you did it for love," Bender snarled. "If you'd stayed to home where you belong this might have ironed itself out. Even if I managed to get him stopped now it wouldn't help your old man. We had a chance to beat Lasham but you threw it away—"

"*I* threw it away!"

"Hell. Can't you *see* it?"

"All I can see," she cried with eyes blazing, "is that broad stripe of yellow you've got running up your back!"

In that luminous half light peculiar to the desert he considered her without expression. Then he picked up his reins. "Tell your father I'm sorry about the way this had to end—"

"It hasn't ended," she said, "and you're not running out." In the stars' pallid gleam he caught the shine of her pistol. "You're going right back there with me. Now rattle your hocks."

9 | THE TASTE OF SWEAT

THEY got in before daylight.

Though plagued by hunger and angered by the knowledge of the girl's continued vigilance, Bender had done a heap of thinking. It had been a cold ride and he climbed down bone weary, staggering a bit with saddle cramp, as he handed the reins to a sleepy-eyed *mozo*.

He followed the girl into the house without speaking and wolfed down the food she put before him in the kitchen, ignoring her silent regard as he ate it. He dippered a drink from the bucket that stood full on the sink, eyeing her across it. "You can go on to bed. I ain't fixin' to leave here."

"Keep your voice down," she said. "I want you to listen to me a minute."

They hadn't turned up any lamps but he could see her well enough by the moonlight flooding in off the patio. She must have been near as dragged out as he was but you'd never get next to that notion just seeing her. She was a hell of a lot of woman any way you wanted to figure it.

"Since we've lost that land we were going to give you I suppose it's about time to reach a new understanding." She watched for his reaction but his face remained like rock.

He didn't say anything. He put the dipper back in the bucket and fished his shirt for the makings, shaping up a smoke as though indifferent to her inspection.

"You'd probably like to get back in cows," she said with the edge of a smile on her lips. "After all, you must want to look forward to something. A man in your fix—"

64

"Never mind about me. You've got all you can handle lookin' out for your own fix."

"Yes . . . but I've something to bargain with. Would a halfway split in this ranch satisfy you?"

"I don't need any bribe to throw a fight at Deef Lasham!"

"But you'll fight a lot harder if you've got a stake in it."

He went over to the stove and found a match. When he looked at her again his eyes were like agate. "I don't know what kind of a jigger you're huntin' but it's damn plain—"

"Let's put it this way," she said, getting out of her chair. "We're an old and proud line, not the kind of a family which likes to accept favors. We'd sooner lose Tres Pinos—"

"You're goin' to lose it, all right! You can make up your mind to that. Nothin' short of an army will keep Deef Lasham from goin' through here just about as he pleases."

He blew smoke through his nose and made a black blob of the butt on his plate. "I'm going to tell you something. You don't have to hold no bait out to me. I'll buck these sheep, but I'll do it on my *own terms* or I ride straight out of this mess tonight."

She stood watching him a moment, the swell of her breasts squeezed tight against her shirtfront. It was hard for him to guess if she were frightened now or furious.

There was nothing but contempt in her voice when she said, "I thought we should get to this finally. Go ahead and make your pitch."

Glaring, Bender rammed big fists in his pockets as though half afraid he might take a swing at her. He started to go without speaking but the scorn of her red lips swung him around. "When I talk turkey," he snarled, "it won't be with no petticoat. Maybe you can make your old man jump through hoops but you ain't about to make no trained seal outa me!"

She didn't move aside, didn't appear to move at all, but suddenly he became uncomfortably conscious of her body. Something strong and unsettling ran vividly between them and he watched those jutting breasts in the lift and fall of her breathing.

He reached out and hauled her toward him. He could feel

her thighs hot against his own. Her lips flattened under his mouth and came apart and the tips of her fingers dug into his shoulders. Time stood still and then she shoved him away.

Against the whiteness of her cheeks her mouth made full and crimson contrast. She said in an outraged breath: "Are those your terms?"

Bender wheeled with a savage fury, too wild to trust his voice with an answer. He crossed the patio, spurs clanking angrily, and went through to the *parada,* jerking open the door to the bunkhouse and standing there a moment like some dark Nemesis, raggedly listening to the sounds of those within.

When he closed the door he had himself in hand again but his face was still turbulent with the violence of his thoughts. Finally he let his breath out and went back across the patio and into his room without a glance at Blanca's door.

HE woke up in the shank of the afternoon, feeling more like himself, and washed at the basin. He slicked back his hair with his fingers and gave some study to the face in his mirror, not particularly pleased with the visage that stared back at him. If he let his whiskers grow it might stall off for awhile those who didn't know him well, but saying "To hell with it!" he shaved. They would find him soon enough if they really made up their minds to.

He got into his shirt, cuffed the dust from his levis and put on his hat. He looked awhile at his shell belt and gun-weighted holster but left them where they hung on the chair-back.

The patio was patterned with sunlight and shadow and over by the coolness of a flowering *palo verde* he saw Don Leo watching the birds about the fountain. The old man smiled and waved him over, inquiring after his health in the gracious Mexican manner. He answered, asked how things were with his host, and then the *ranchero* said, "I was told you were back. I have been waiting for a word with you."

Avoiding the barrel, Bender said, "Too bad about that land."

Don Leo shrugged. "What is spilled cannot be returned to the bottle. All is not yet lost, however. I still have Tres Pinos and if you will see me through this trouble, *amigo,* one half of it and half of all my cattle will be your share when this thing has been finished."

"The picture's changed," Bender grunted. "We had a fifty-fifty chance when we started but Hazel's coup has knocked that in the head and Blanca, breaking me out of that jail, has put this spread right where Lasham wants it. Sure, I'm willing to admit they may not have got onto her, but they know from her voice it was a woman got me out. You better pull in your horns and let his sheep go through—"

"Never!" Don Leo cried fiercely.

"Well," Bender shrugged, "I guess you know what'll happen. He'll go through this spread with every sheep he can get hold of and when he gets done you won't have enough feed to chink the ribs of a locust. Let him pass without hindrance and you'll still have the land—"

"Of what good is land without honor?" Don Leo grumbled. "No, my friend, we may be whipped as you say, we may even lose everything, but we will fight to the end. We will fight, *senor*, till there is none left among us but no *Texano* shall ever say a Lopez was afraid!"

His curly beard bristled and he scowled like an angry eagle, but the spirit was stronger than the flesh it reposed in and, after a moment, he sank back in his chair, mumbling and muttering impotently in Spanish.

Bender glowered too but he nursed his hate in silence. And then the old man said, "Please understand, I wish you to stay here—"

"Look," Bender growled. "I've been publicly arrested—I'm a fugitive wanted for murder. You want them bastards to hang it on you? That's what they'll do if I stay here. They'll brand this spread—"

"No matter. I want you to stay and take charge of this fighting. Ask what you will—"

"All right, I'll stay. But on one condition. That I have complete charge. That what I say goes until we're done one way or the other with Lasham."

Don Leo, peering up at him anxiously, nodded. *"Seguro, si,"* he said, and gave Walt Bender his hand.

THEY sat a brief while in silence then, Bender pulling his notions together. There were still several things he didn't properly understand, but one thing he knew beyond question —he couldn't go at this with wraps on. In the bunkhouse, for instance, there'd be a heap of resentment. There would undoubtedly be times when the old man would wish he'd never heard of Walt Bender. This was a job for Simon Legree.

He got up, saying briskly, "The most of them ought to be in by now so we may as well get the ball to rolling. I want you to tell them I'm the new general manager."

Don Leo sighed and led the way to the *parada*. Several of the men were busy caring for the horses but he beckoned them away and called the rest from their quarters. In Spanish he told them about the threat of the sheep and introduced Bender as the new *majordomo*. "His word in all things will be final."

Bender, studying their faces, stepped forward as he finished.

"Don Leo has told me he has fourteen cowboys. I count fourteen noses. Who, then, is watching the cattle?"

He threw the question at Gonzales and saw the man's eyes widen. In a tone barely bordering on civility the redheaded foreman said it wasn't their custom to watch the cattle at night.

"Then we'll change the custom," Bender told him. "Perhaps in the old days that style was okay; cattle weren't worth so much a man would mind losing a few off and on. But the price has gone up. There are gringos in the country now and we adopt gringo ways or we don't stay in business. You will divide the crew in relays and make sure that six men are with the cattle always. In the night they'll be close-herded and at the least sign of trouble one man will ride the fastest horse and come at once to report it. Is that clear, Pedrocito?"

Gonzales' eyes, turned narrow, swung a look at Don Leo and came sullenly back. He jerked his face in a nod. And then he scowled and spat disgustedly.

"Also," Bender said, ignoring this, "you will keep two men continually on watch at that shack above the bluffs. At the first appearance of sheep on the desert one will fetch the word while the other remains to keep an eye on developments. And mark this well: no stranger is to pass or be allowed to approach the *casa* without I have okayed him."

He looked them over again, beckoning one from the line, an old dark-faced fellow with a large bristling mustache and a neck criss-crossed with the creases of time and weather. Holding his hat in his hand he met Bender's eye without fear or favor.

"What's your name?" Bender asked.

"Jose Maria Roblero, *senor*."

"Well, Jose," Bender said, "do you think you could hitch up a team and drive a wagon?"

The old man's eyes crinkled with laughter. "I think I could do that, yes."

Bender nodded. "There are coyotes around these parts, Jose. I think we should lay in a large supply of strychnine. Do you think you could take this wagon into Afton and fetch back about thirty sacks of the stuff?"

The old man looked a little startled for a moment, then he bobbed his head.

"That's fine," Bender said. "Suppose you get right at it. Oh —and Jose! Better fetch a few hundred Colt and Winchester cartridges. Some of these coyotes we might have to kill by hand."

When the old man had taken himself off to catch the team up, Bender's eyes searched out Scar Face. He looked at him so long the man at last began to squirm. Then Bender said without preface: "You sleep all right last night?"

The bravo's face wrinkled up into an expression of puzzlement but the mismatched eyes clouded over and turned watchful. "Sure," he said. "All the time I sleep good——"

"Where?"

The fellow jerked a thumb toward the men's quarters back of him.

Bender shook his head. "Not last night you didn't."

"Oh—last night! No. I see my wife. In Columbus. She going to have the baby."

Gonzales spoke up. "He had my permission——"

"Nobody's talking to you." Bender watched Scar Face's eyes getting smaller and smaller, saw them drop to his waist and come up again, brightening.

"And yesterday, I suppose, you were watching the cattle."

Scar Face shrugged. "Every day I watch the cows."

The jingle and scrape of Bender's big-roweled spurs flung out bleak vibrations as he walked up to the man, crowding him away from the advantage of the wall, and forcing him to turn until he could not see Gonzales. "If there's one thing I never been able to abide it's a goddam belly-crawling sidewinding liar. You never went near Columbus last night!"

Out of the shocked stillness Gonzales' voice cried harshly: "How can you know where this man was?"

"Sheriff found me, didn't he?"

Don Leo peered at Bender incredulously. "Are you trying to tell me this man is a spy?"

"Do I have to?" Bender countered. "Hasn't it struck you as odd that pair should have arrived so opportunely at a moment when nothing else could have saved Block 10 for Deef Lasham? That they came with drawn guns and knew right where to find me?"

"But," declared Gonzales, "it was not Fentress who found you. It was this other one, this Red Hat, that told him who you were."

"And," Scar Face sneered, "it was after Esteban sent Eusebio—" He broke off abruptly, his whole look stiffening.

Bender's hard teeth gleamed behind tight lips.

The Mexican, knowing he was trapped, abruptly flung himself at Bender with a kill-crazy snarl. A knife flashed in his hand, its honed blade glinting wickedly. But the Texan, expecting this, ducked the murderous slash and put four knuckles hard against the fellow's chin.

The Mexican's head was slammed sideways. The knife fell out of his paralyzed fingers. For a moment he hung there, teetering wildly, falling suddenly backwards. His shoulders struck like a burst sack.

Bender stepped into the bunkhouse. He came out with a

bucket, splashed the contents over the prostrate man and watched him come spluttering up on an elbow.

"Get onto your feet!"

The man rolled his eyes like a stallion bronc. He levered his back up off of the ground, got a knee planted under him and went for his gun.

Bender stood blackly watching. He waited till the man had almost got the thing from leather then he brought down the bucket, breaking it without mercy on the man's unprotected head.

Breath sighed out of the staring crew.

Bender showed them a tough and thin-stretched smile till their eyes found something better to look at. Several crossed themselves, silently muttering, and the Texan, turning his head, saw that Blanca was standing, shoulders taut, beside her father.

She said in English, "Was that necessary?"

"Maybe you think I should have given him a medal."

"You should have used a little tact. Do you want them to hate you?"

"Should I care about that? I'm buildin' a crew that'll jump when I tell them." He gave her back a look as bleak as her own. "Any time I don't suit, your old man can fire me. Until he does, I'll do the job *my* way. *Agua!*" he snapped, and a man ran to fetch it.

He gave Blanca a knowledgeable grin and watched her eyes flash.

"You're as hateful a man as I have ever encountered," she said with her breath jerking in and out angrily. She turned her back and went over and stood beside the redheaded foreman.

The man who had gone for the water came back with it and, at Bender's nod, sloshed it over Lasham's agent. They got him onto his feet where he stood dripping and miserable, in his wet clothes looking like a half-drowned rat.

When his mismatched eyes swung blearily into focus, Bender said, "Pick up your belongings and go pack the rest of them."

THE crew stood around with expressionless faces while the discharged man threw his gear on a horse. When he came from the house with his bedroll Bender said to Gonzales, "Take a good look at him. He's the one you can thank for losing that grass."

"I hired him," Blanca frowned. "You don't need to blame Pete. He came up off the desert by the same trail you did."

Bender ignored her. The man got on his horse, not quite making it the first time, and rode through the gate. When they couldn't hear the horse any longer Don Leo said wearily, "He will tell that Lasham about this poison you are buying."

"I hope so," Bender nodded. He waved a hand at the men. "Better put on the feed bags. We've got a hard night before us."

He turned to the rancher. "Where's the nearest market? I'm going to round up your beef."

"The nearest market's Deming—but is this wise, do you think? A little later in the season—"

"A little later in the season you won't have anything to market. If *we* don't move them the sheep crowd will. I want that dough you got from Lasham."

Don Leo stood for a long while silent. When he spoke his voice was hardly more than a whisper. "I do not have that money."

"You don't have it!" Bender stared. "What the hell have you done with it?"

Gonzales said, "Coming back from Deming last night I was robbed."

10 | RED HAT

"WELL, isn't that just ducky!"

Gonzales' eyes swiveled away and he hurriedly put more ground between them as though half expecting the gringo to strike him.

Bender stared at the girl, then looked at her father, and it took all the will he had to keep silent. Small wonder the old man was losing his grip. He had known about this when they'd talked in the patio; it was why he had been so anxiously insistent that Bender write his own ticket for this deal. If they couldn't pay off they might not have any ranch!

"When does this money have to be paid back?"

The old man shrugged. He looked stupid.

"On the tenth," Blanca said.

Less than two weeks away!

"And what do you figure to pay it with—peanuts?"

"There are the cattle," she said, her eyes watching him anxiously.

"Yeah," Bender said, "the cattle," and swore. "Get the stuff on the table," he told her gruffly and, turning away from them, clanked into the passage and went scowling across the patio.

He strode into his room and buckled on his shell belt. Then he took out his gun, going over it thoroughly, cleaning it and oiling it and slipping in fresh cartridges. And all this while he kept thinking of Deef Lasham, turning over what he knew, considering other things suspected.

He hadn't any doubt but what Gonzales had been robbed. It was just the kind of stunt that bastard sheep crowd would

73

have thought of. They'd tried it once before only this time they'd got the job done. Had they used Art again or was this some of Hazel's handiwork?

There wasn't much chance he could get it back even if he knew who had taken it, but any kind of chance was better than sitting here.

He picked up his hat and went out to the *comedor*. The food was on the table. Gonzales was drawing his chair up. Don Leo, already seated, was staring unseeingly into his plate and the girl was fixing a snack for her mother.

Bender flung down his hat and dropped into a chair. Hardly waiting for the old man to get done with the blessing, he said grimly to the foreman: "How many of them jumped you?"

"One," Gonzales said.

"Was it Red Hat?"

"How could I know? He wore only a flour sack with holes for his eyes."

"Well, he said something, didn't he? Wouldn't you recognize his voice?"

Gonzales shook his red head.

"Where'd he stop you?"

"In the town," Gonzales grunted. "He was in the mouth of that alley between the Aces Up and the Bottleneck Bar. He told me to drop the money and, when I did, he said 'Now hump it.' "

Pretty slick, Bender thought. A man had to admire its extreme simplicity. It was the kind of a deal that would appeal to Syd Hazel and it had Hazel's boldness.

When they shoved back their chairs and he and the foreman were shaping their smokes up, Don Leo, finally rousing himself, asked hesitantly, "Is there anything we can do?"

Bender scratched a match on the seam of his levis, got his cigarette going and scowled through the smoke. "There's probably a lot of things—if a fellow could think of them."

"I went back after awhile," Gonzales said.

"Did you go into those dives?"

"Into both of them, yes. But I didn't know who to look for.

I did not see this man of the red sombrero. A fat man was playing cards at a table with the sheriff and two others."

That fetched Bender's head around. Gonzales nodded. "It was the man who gave me the money. Lasham."

Bender stubbed out his smoke and picked up his hat. "Post two men at that shack. Take the rest of the crew and start rounding up cattle—round up everything wearing the Three Pines brand. I'll be back, like enough, before you've got the herd ready; but if I'm not, start the drive and keep your eye peeled for trouble."

"Where are you going?"

It was Blanca, coming back from the bedroom with her mother's empty dishes. She asked him again, and there was something in her look that made him—just a moment—wonder.

Then he shoved the thought aside. "I'm going after that money," he said, and departed.

IT was ten fifteen by the fly speckled clock above O'Cleary's bar when Cash Fentress stepped through the green-painted batwings and, cutting a way through the crowd with his shoulders, dropped into a chair at an empty table that was placed one stride from the closed side door.

This table, its location and his own presence at it were familiar facets of the dive's nightly ritual. Blue smoke patterned the air beneath the hanging lanterns and a steady drone of talk made soothing background for the clack of chips and the chants of the housemen. This was the part of his day most enjoyed by the sheriff and he looked around with approval as he imagined the money rolling into O'Cleary's till. There were bottles on most of the tables, the bar was packed three deep and the games looked to be in a satisfactory state of progress.

These appearances put the lawman in a mellow frame of mind for he had this big Irishman right where he wanted him and the more the man made the bigger the take that was in it for Fentress. Silent partner was a role he played very well as others besides O'Cleary could have bitterly attested; and now he was about ready to move in on Red Hat.

He hadn't yet discovered what Syd Hazel was up to but it was certainly something crooked. Setting up a dummy to bid in Indian grass was a business sure to be frowned on if it were brought to the government's notice; and there was also that business of Bender. It all added up to what should be a sizeable profit soon as he learned enough of the background to understand where to put the squeeze. Perhaps he could get it hooked up tonight. The man should be dropping in pretty soon.

He glanced again at the clock and got out a cigar. He was biting the end off when the side door opened. He wasn't facing the door but he felt its brief draft and supposed this was Hazel.

Fellow'd certainly been in no lather to get here!

Fentress dug up a match without looking around, snapped a light on his thumbnail and waggled it in front of his smoke with much ceremony. Let the sonofabitch wait!

When the match was about finished he shook it out and looked up.

Instead of seeing the man he'd expected, he found Walt Bender standing over him. He did a quick double take and nearly choked with the shock of it.

Bender grinned toothily. "Push over," he said.

It went through Fentress' mind to start raising the roof but a second covert look at Bender's eyes derailed the impulse.

He got up as though hypnotized. "Not there," Bender growled. "Plunk your can down where you can look at the wall. You won't be so tempted to commit suicide that way."

Like a man on stilts the sheriff moved over and eased himself down like he was squatting on a time bomb.

Bender slid into the vacated chair.

During the following uncomfortable silence the walls, the room and its gabbling customers seemed to feather away like sun-cut mist, leaving only the table and that Texan's hard stare. Fentress' world wouldn't swing into proper focus. It just didn't make sense a guy wanted for murder could be such a fool as to come here and sit down with the man he'd just got away from.

"Kind of queer, ain't it?" Bender said conversationally—
"damn near as queer as you lettin' me get out of there. Only
that ain't queer to me. I savvy that part plenty."

He leaned abruptly forward, whispering weirdly, "Happens
sometimes like that to the best of us."

Fentress occasionally had nightmares, but nothing like this.
His throat was like cotton. He licked at his lips. He had to
lick them again before he could manage to say, "What does?"

The words came out in a hoarse kind of croak.

"Getting caught in a crack. Feelin' it closing in on you."

Bender's teeth gleamed again in a horrible grimace and
he signaled a waiter, ordering some beer—"In a bottle," he
specified.

The man came and fetched it and drifted away.

Bender said, reflective like, "I've seen critters do some queer
things in a trap . . . Some rats will gnaw their legs off. Snap
their bones in their teeth just like you'd snap a match stick.
Go crazy, I guess."

He poured some beer in his glass but made no move to
pick the glass up. "Reckon whatever they give you must have
looked just like gravy. It most generally does in a case of that
kind. No trouble, no fuss; a chunk to add to the nest egg. Only
when you lap gravy," he said, suddenly savage, "you want to
wipe off your mouth!"

The sheriff was a fish abruptly jerked out of water. He
gasped and he goggled.

"You're in a bad spot, Fentress." Bender eased the table
toward him, making himself more room behind it, letting his
right hand drop below its ledge out of sight. "You've got a
bear by the tail and now it's your move again."

The sheriff drew a long breath but it didn't thaw out the
cold lump in his larynx. He shook in his boots like a man with
the ague. It didn't help him to know that all this guy'd said
was a bunch of damned words, that nothing had changed but
his view of this business. Treacherous himself he expected
treachery in others and what Bender'd said rang a loud bell of
warning. He could call out for help—and he would probably

get it—but the both of them knew he wasn't about to. Not with that hand underneath the table.

Bender's eyes held the shine of old cinch rings. "You're a sittin' duck, Fentress. They've got you out in the cold and lonesome. You gave 'em the lever when you lugged me off to that foolproof jail and let me get loose."

"Hell's afire!" Fentress snarled. "Say what you mean an' quit beatin' the bushes. If—"

Bender's smile broke his words off. Bender's eyes, moving up and just a fraction away from him, were looking toward the door with the most pleased expression they had shown in a long while. "Come right in," he said heartily—"come right in and sit yourself down."

His hidden hand moved briefly, his left boot thrust a chair out. Fentress, goosey as a schoolgirl, twisted his head and saw Red Hat standing like a glowering bull behind him.

Hazel seemed to be having a little trouble with his breathing. The sheriff felt for him, but not very much. He said, "Yes. By *all* means. I've got a few things to say to you myself."

"Relax," Red Hat said, "he ain't goin' to kill no one." He swung the pushed-out chair around; sat down with its back in front of him. "What's stuck in *your* craw?" He flung the brusque words at Bender.

"A little matter," Bender said, "of forty-five hundred dollars."

"Do I look like a walkin' bank?" Hazel sneered.

Bender's hand made a movement underneath the table. "Cough up—an' quick."

His eyes were polished glass, without expression.

Hazel's burly shoulders rose in a shrug. "Always glad to help a friend," he drawled, grinning sourly, and thrust his left paw at his left hip pocket, at the same time lunging across the back of the chair in a forward dive that carried everything before it.

The table went over with a hell of a crash. Bender's gun went off and Fentress screamed like a hog.

11 | THE MUSCLE
MEN

THERE wasn't anything wrong with him a drink wouldn't cure, but you'd have thought the way he lay there in that twichery heap he'd been salivated surely and was dying now by inches.

Bender, also on the floor, discovered that time could be elastic. With Fentress' uproar jerking at his nerves, it seemed to take forever to get himself untangled from the wreckage of that chair, to roll and come up on two knees and an elbow —even his pistol seemed to fire by slow motion.

Actually his movements had a speed little slower than lightning. He got in the first shot—even triggered a second at Red Hat crouched behind the overturned table before anyone else got a gun into action. Then he flung himself upright and lunged for the door.

Behind him everyone was shouting at once. Questions and orders and curses all were scrambled in a deafening racket and some damn fool was blasting the door full of peepholes, but he got the thing open and stumbled outside.

After that bright blaze of lights this alley looked dark as a stack of fresh-blacked stove lids. There was a very present danger he might trip and go down—about a five-to-three chance if you wanted the odds on it—but this wasn't any time to be worrying about intangibles. He tore through the murk like a bat out of Carlsbad, trying to get around the corner before that bunch came through the door.

He pretty nearly did it. He was within two strides of cutting it when the guns opened up behind him. He caught the thin whine of unseen bullets; in these narrow confines the reports of those shots were like rocks coming down off a cliff in spring thaw. And then he was around the corner and the night was less black and he was safe for the moment.

He pulled a ragged breath deep into his lungs. His horse was still tethered under the branches of a tamarisk thirty feet away. The big dun was watching him nervously, fretful and alarmed by the continuing racket. Bender went over to him, murmuring soothingly, unknotted the reins and then paused, not quite decided. He was loath to go off without recovering that money.

He led the horse around and tied him back of the tamarisk. There were a bunch of beer and whisky kegs stacked up behind the back end of the building and a low shed roof coming out just above them. A hunch sent him toward them and in a matter of seconds he was on the shed roof, considering the second story's two black windows. He listened a moment, hearing nothing from the alley but a mutter of voices. On hands and knees he went up the roof's incline, rose carefully before the nearest window and tried it. The lower sash wasn't locked and he shoved it up quickly, mainly concerned with getting himself out of sight. As he thrust a leg over the sill he heard the sheriff's voice in the alley.

He swung himself through and quietly closed the window. He couldn't see a thing and he crouched there, breath jammed, while he strained his ears to catch other breathing. Satisfied he was alone, he stretched out his left hand until his fingers touched a wall. Moving slowly and cautiously he felt his way around it, coming finally to the door. He pressed an ear flat against it but he didn't hear any movement.

He tried to put himself in Red Hat's place, wondering what the man would do. It didn't seem at all likely Lasham's sheep boss would bother to do anything. The burden of action rested squarely on Fentress. To make things look right the sheriff would probably swear in a posse and go through the motions of making a search. At least, Bender hoped he would; and the bigger the posse the better he'd like it.

With all the stealth he could muster, Bender opened the door. The barroom sounds were much plainer now; he could even make out occasional snatches of talk. A flight of stairs led sharply down at his left. There was a door at the bottom with light splintering through the cracks in its panel. To Bender's right a narrow hall went to a window at the front; the blind was pulled down but light from the street came in around its edges, enough for him to see three other doors opening off the hall. There was light under the middle one; he didn't hear any voices.

He still hadn't figured how he would get hold of Hazel. Even if he dared lurk at that window a view of the street wouldn't be much good to him if Red Hat decided to depart via the alley. One of these other rooms might have a window on the alley but to watch that alley exclusively could hardly be any better and, if these rooms did not happen to be regularly occupied, there was the considerable risk he might be detected by whoever was in that room with the light.

He scowled through the gloom, bitterly considering a new thought. Hazel, if he hadn't already nipped off, might be planning to wait for the return of the sheriff.

There could be no profit in Bender waiting that long. If he was going to get out of here now was the time.

He started back into the room, abruptly stopped and looked back toward the room with the light. He had no damned reason for thinking such a thought but it was in his mind Deef Lasham might be in there and he was pulled toward it strongly. It would be a hell of a lot easier to get the money from Lasham than it would trying to take it away from Syd Hazel.

Just the thought of Deef Lasham was enough to stir sparks from the hot core of anger that was smoldering in Bender. He had the sheep king to thank for everything that had happened to him and he stepped back in the hall again, glaring at the crack of light that came from under that closed middle door. If this wasn't Lasham's room, or if the fat toad wasn't in there, the only alternative that crossed his mind—short of going back to Three Pines without accomplishing anything—was to go on downstairs and try another whack at Hazel.

Bender, grating his teeth, was starting toward the middle

door when light, with an uprush of sound from the barroom, fanned out across the ceiling and, with an equal abruptness, vanished. The stairs creaked under a heavy tread and Bender, smothering a bitter curse, again backed into the room he had come out of, flattening himself against the wall, not daring to shut the door lest it screak.

The boots reached the top of the stairs and stopped. Bender, holding his breath, could visualize the fellow warily eyeing that open door. The boots moved again, coming cautiously nearer. A hand reached out, the door swayed and groaned, and through the hinged crack he could see the black shape of the man's hatted head.

Bender's heart started knocking. The need to breathe was sheer torture. Every nerve pulled tight and trembled, and just as Bender felt he couldn't any longer stand it the head was withdrawn and the boots moved up the hall.

Mere air had never tasted one half as good. It was like some heady elixir, and Bender thought he never could gulp in enough of it but he forgot all about such abstractions as breathing when light targeted the man moving into that middle room.

Red Hat!

There was no doubt about it; the guy was Syd Hazel. Bender heard the muffled growl of his voice as the closing door blanked out the light.

Like a stalking cat he was out in the hall with his ear to that door before Hazel got seated—he even heard the chair scrape as the sheep boss dropped into it.

Now was the chance to overhear a little something that might give him a clue to what the sheep crowd was planning; but even as the thought went through his head Bender was reaching for the knob, knowing he didn't have the time.

He flung the door open and stepped in, gun in hand.

He'd guessed right about one thing; it was Lasham's room. The sheep king was seated beside a roll-top desk. His jowled face quivered around like an over heaped plate of jello. His mouth fell open and his eyes looked like they would roll off his cheekbones.

Bender, staring at the man, simply couldn't understand it. Ever since that day back in Texas when the sheep king had framed him with the killing of Toby Bronsen, he had never thought of anything he would like half so well as to get his two hands wrapped around this fat hog's neck. He had ridden a thousand miles with that picture, had dreamed a million times of just how he would do it—and now that, at last, he had come up with the bastard all he could feel was a nauseous contempt.

Why, the fool was half out of his mind with fright! He had built Bender into such a fire-breathing monster he had come to the point where he believed those lies himself.

Just looking at the fellow made him feel like puking. He said, "I'm not going to waste any time with you, Lasham. Your handyman here"—he jerked his gun snout at Hazel—"lifted forty-five hundred off Gonzales last night. I want it back. Right now."

The fat man's cheeks were gray as ashes. With shaking hands he peeled the bills off his roll.

"Now add another five thousand for that range you ruined for me."

More bills fell to increase the pile on the desk top.

"Dig out a clean sheet of paper. Get a pen and some ink." He kicked the door shut with his heel while he watched Deef Lasham do this. "Now put down what I tell you. To whom it may concern: I, Aaron Abijah Lasham, knowing that Toby Bronsen, the Texas senator, was about to tell his constituents I had been paying him large sums of money to put through legislation advantageous to sheep and particularly to the sheep pool with which I am connected, did wilfully and deliberately, on the occasion of the Labor Day rally at Kermit, put a forty-five slug between his eyes at close quarters. I make this confession for the good of my soul, which same may God take mercy on.

"Now sign it," Bender grated, "and get over against that wall."

Red Hat looked at his boss incredulously. "You're a fool if you give him a thing like that—tear it up!" he snarled.

But the fat man signed it, staggered out of his chair, put his belly against the wall and thrust both hands above his head.

Bender focused the gun on Lasham's gaping *segundo*. "I'll want your signature as witness—"

"You can go right on a-wantin'."

There was a cold hard watchfulness in the look Bender slanched at Hazel. "I'm not figuring to stand any foolishness from you. At the first sign of trouble I'm going to smash both your elbows. Now get out of that gun belt."

Red Hat looked at him toughly. "Take your dough an' git goin'—you ain't shootin' nobody. You know what'd happen if you let off that popgun. Half the boys in that bar would come poundin' up them stairs."

"They won't be much comfort to a busted arm. For the last time I'm telling you: Unbuckle that gun belt."

Red Hat settled himself like a millstone. His cat's yellow eyes loosed a glow of derision. "Hell with you," he said; and Bender squeezed the trigger.

THE sheriff, Cash Fentress, had a lot more wheels in his thinkbox than either side in this ruckus had given him credit for. His dive for the floor and subsequent howling was a fine bit of acting designed not only to keep the gunfire away from him but to lower his importance in the minds of those who witnessed it. He wasn't near as scared as he made himself out to be and when, after Bender's hurried exit, Syd Hazel's scathing words reminded him of his duties he put on another good show of shudderingly pulling himself together. When it was amply apparent Bender'd gotten away he went blustering out and swore in a posse. He put the town barber in charge of this outfit and told him to case all the trails leading north. "This feller's dangerous—don't take any chances. If you cut his sign send somebody after me. While you're gone I'll be combin' the town."

He didn't care what they thought; he wanted only to be rid of them. As soon as they'd climbed into saddles and gone, he got his own horse and rode off east of town into the region of shacks given over to section hands, teamsters and other personnel commonly employed by the railroad. He knew the place that he wanted but he spent several minutes angling cautiously around to make certain he wasn't followed. Finally convinced, he took off his badge and slipped it into his pocket, loosened the gun in his holster and, softly whistling the *Cowboy's Lament,* moved leisurely up to a decrepit unpainted shanty whose yard was cluttered with a bunch of chicken coops.

Several birds started squawking as he got out of the saddle. There were blankets over the windows and no sign of light. He knocked three times and growled, "I wanta buy some chickens," before he got any answer. Then a gruff voice grumbled, "Wait'll I git on my pants," and Fentress, scowling with impatience, snarled, "The girls don't wear pants where I come from."

The door was whisked open and he stepped inside.

"Don't you ever get tired of all this damn tomfoolery?"

Art Chesseldine chuckled. "What you got on your mind?"

He had a round long jaw and ears that stuck out like handles. His bulging forehead was sheathed in sandy short cut hair and the big-jawed face was unlined and ruddy. He didn't look to be over twenty-two or twenty-three but was solidly built, heavily muscled and swell-chested, with a huge pair of hands that could have twisted bar iron. It was hard in the smoky light of that lantern to be sure of his expression but the sheriff wasn't letting that stand in the way of what he had come for.

"You know any guy named Bender—Walt Bender?"

"I've heard," Art said, "that he got out of your jail."

"He got out," Fentress growled, "because I was well paid to let him."

"I kind of figured that out. Pretty well heeled, eh?"

Fentress brushed that aside. "I found out most of this after it was over. A rough lookin' gent in a red hat come after me; said there was a guy at the auction that was wanted in Texas— wanted five hundred bucks worth; an escaped murderer, he tells me. So I pull the guy in. Then this Red Hat, later, slips

me double the bounty to look the other way while this Bender
gets loose."

"Must of taken some doin'."

"Some dame got him out. I want to know who she was."

"So now I'm a mind reader." Chesseldine grinned.

"You can tell me, all right. There's somethin' damn big
gettin' ready to break here an' when it tears loose I want to be
in on it."

"You better talk to this Red Hat—"

"Wait a minute," Fentress said, "I'm goin' to show you the
angles. Yesterday Esteban, a guy with more debts than he's
got buttons on his clothes, shows up at that auction and bids
in a big bunch of land, payin' cash. At the time I show up,
fetched by Red Hat, this Bender's outbid him on a block that
joins Tres Pinos, a tamale outfit south of the Floridas. Red
Hat calls the turn on Bender, I lug him off and the spik gets
the land—that make any sense to you?"

Chesseldine shrugged.

The sheriff said, "I don't catch it right off. But when Red
Hat slips me double the bounty to keep outa the way while this
dame springs Bender, things begins to add up."

"You figure this bird put up the dough?"

"He's slipperier'n a basket of snakes, I'll say that much. He
shows me a dodger an' gets action on Bender. My juggin'
Bender lets that land go to Esteban. When the Mex gets the
land our red-hatted friend should of been done with Bender,
but instead he pays me double what I could of cashed the
guy in for. Just to keep outa my office for awhile. Is this guy
ackshully Bender or ain't he? If he is, why bail him out?
Why bail him out *anyway?* And where's the girl fit into this?
An' who the hell *is* she?"

Chesseldine considered the sheriff without comment. He
rasped a hand across his jaw, got up and turned down the
wick of the smoking lantern.

"An' here's another odd thing," Fentress growled. "Tonight
I'm sittin' in the Aces Up, havin' my evenin' smoke like
usual, when in walks Bender. He comes in that side door right
alongside my table and sits himself down just as cool as a well

chain. He feeds me some guff about bein' a settin' duck. Red Hat shows his mug about then an' Bender jumps him, tellin' him to shell out forty-five hundred. There's a ruckus, of course. Bender gets away—I'm supposed to be huntin' him now with a posse."

"Busy night," Art offered.

"That all you can say?"

"What'd you want me to say?"

Fentress, scowling, climbed out of his chair. He banged a fist down so hard on Chesseldine's table it made the dirty dishes jump. "I got a gold mine here if I can find the damn vein!"

"So I should turn cartwheels mebbe?"

"I need help," Fentress grumbled.

"So I rake in the chestnuts while you sit back an' eat 'em. No thanks."

Their eyes locked and held. The sheriff said, "I need your boys, Art. I'll take the bite off your rustlin' an' cut you in for half of every damn dollar we get out of this deal. Does that sound?"

"I can't hear it."

Fentress' cheeks turned dark with anger. "What the hell do you want?"

"You think my bunch is goin' to work at this for nothing? I want it split three ways—"

"Two for you, eh?"

"One for me, one for you, and one for the boys that'll be takin' the chances."

Fentress' twisted mouth showed the tumult inside him. Art Chesseldine's face was like the side of a mountain. Fentress said, voice tight with fury, "I let you in on—"

"You ain't lettin' me in on a goddam thing! I was workin' on this before you ever got wind of it."

"Says you!" Fentress sneered.

"You can take it or leave it."

Fentress had no real choice and he was smart enough to know it; he'd suspected all along that this damn rustler was in it someplace. "All right," he said finally, putting the best face he could on it, "we split the take three ways—now let's hear what you know."

"First," said Art, grinning, "I'll take my two-thirds of what you got from Hazel on Bender."

For a number of pregnant moments it looked as though Cash Fentress was about to burst his surcingle. But he got hold of himself, managing to keep the hot words jammed inside him, very probably helped by the knowledge implied in Chesseldine's use of Red Hat's name. With his eyes winnowed down to glittering slits he counted out the rustler's cut and flung the bills down on the table in silence.

"Bender's wanted, all right," Art said calmly. "I'm not sure just yet where he comes into this thing but I've had a man back in Texas and it seems Bender killed a senator called Bronsen. After Bender ducked out his cattle disappeared and Lasham sheeped off what was left of his range. This redhatted Syd Hazel is Deef Lasham's sheep boss and the money Esteban used to bid in them lease lands probably come from Lasham."

"Bender was tryin' to get himself another start in the cow business, you think?"

Chesseldine shrugged. "I think he was bidding on Block 10 for Tres Pinos. I think Lasham's moving in here. Red Hat arranged with me to see that Lopez, who owns Three Pines, got to know about that auction. He's got his range overstocked and could use some extra grass, but he ain't got the cash to go bid at that auction. So I tell him where he can get it and Lasham loans him forty-five hundred. On a short term note."

Fentress considered this. "Never, of course, havin' any intention of lettin' Don Leo bid in that grass. What Lasham was after was a right-of-way through the old man's place. But how did Bender get into that biddin'? I wouldn't think he'd—"

"He's been holed up at Tres Pinos."

"The old man's been hidin' him?"

Chesseldine spat. "You could call it that, I reckon. He's been livin' in the house; gave him the room right next the girl."

Fentress looked at him carefully. "You must have got damn close to know that much."

"I had a man planted on 'em. A spik. In the outfit."

The sheriff looked interested. "What else have you learned?"

"They've made Bender manager, right over Gonzales' head. First thing he did was send a wagon after strychnine."

"They're goin' to fight Lasham then." Fentress swore. He said disgustedly, "Lasham's movin' in. He's fetchin' his sheep across that desert an' the shortest way to get them on this grass is through Three Pines." He scowled at the money he'd flung down beside the dishes.

Chesseldine nodded. "Nothing in that for us."

"You don't look disappointed enough. Kick in," Fentress scowled. "What's the rest of it?"

"Well, it looks like to me that that's about the size of it. It looks like the sheep crowd's tryin' to rub off some of Bender's rep on Lopez or—which amounts to the same thing —on his ranch. That's all he's got that I ever heard of. Figurin' they'll fight, Lasham's tryin' to use Bender to discredit 'em 'fore they get started. Then he'll call on you to keep order and allow him passage and, when you can't do it, he'll use Bender's presence as an excuse to call in the Cavalry."

Fentress chewed at his lip. "There's got to be somethin' else," he said doggedly, and Chesseldine nodded. "It just don't stand to reason," Fentress snarled, "that any tight-fisted skunk with the rep Lasham got would be throwin' his money around like water if all he was after is a bunch of damn grass!"

Chesseldine said, "It's knowing Deef Lasham that sticks in my craw. I knew him over in Texas when he didn't have a pot and from all that I've heard he ain't changed any. There's two hundred thousand acres of Indian grass in them leases and, countin' Block 10, he didn't bid in more than half of it, probably figurin' to steal the rest. But—and this is the part I keep stumblin' over—it's the first time that bastard ever paid cash for anything! So why did he do it?"

"Let's consider what it gets him."

"No secret about that. It gets him the chance to spread his

damn sheep clean across the whole business. There ain't none
of it fenced an' he'll claim he couldn't hold them."

"Sure," Fentress said, "but it gives him more reason for
crossin' Tres Pinos. Just like the note he holds for that loan.
With the note *and* them leases there ain't a court in the
country would blame him for takin' his sheep through that
ranch."

"Which brings us right back to Bender," Chesseldine
grimaced. "Lasham *wanted* Bender loose. He *wanted* Blanca
Lopez to spring him. He wants Bender publicly tied in with
that outfit."

"I'll buy that," Fentress nodded.

"Then it leaves us right smack out in the cold. Because,
if that much is true, all Lasham's after is that grass."

"He could be after the land—"

"He's only got the land *leased*."

"I was thinkin' about Tres Pinos. . . ."

"Tres Pinos!" Chesseldine snorted. "There ain't enough
grass on that spread to—"

"Maybe," Fentress scowled, "that's been our trouble. We
keep thinkin' of grass but it could be somethin' else."

"Sure. A gold mine, mebbe."

But the sheriff wasn't laughing. He was staring intently
into the flame of the smoky lantern, his thoughtfully narrowed
eyes gone hours away from this confab. "There was a guy in
the land office goin' through the records. . . ."

Chesseldine came off the bunk like a cat. He caught Fentress' shoulder, savagely shaking him. "When?"

"Couple of weeks ago. One mornin'. Early. Big sloppy
jasper with a cud in one cheek an' a oversized belly—"

"My Gawd! Lasham!"

12 | ALARMS AND EXCURSIONS

EVEN as the jarring crash of that shot slammed against the walls and came racketing back, Bender knew with a nightmare sense of panic any chance he had left would have to hinge on split seconds.

There was no time to think, no time to do anything; yet he could not, would not, go without that paper which might be no good at all to him unless he could make Syd Hazel sign it.

Against the wall Lasham's shape was grotesque with shudders. Shock had twisted Red Hat's face and above the ghastly cheeks his eyes were wild with a murderous fury as Bender jerked him wickedly out of his chair and flung him with no care at all toward the desk. Hazel bared his teeth but, with the snout of Bender's gun staring at him, he bent over the desk and picked up Lasham's pen.

Bender tore the sixshooter out of his holster and flung it under the rumpled bed. "Down at the bottom write 'witness' and sign it."

Red Hat leaned with one hip braced against the soiled wood and, half crazed with pain, scrawled his name left-handed while shouts from below came up through the flooring and blood dripped redly into the carpet from the useless fingers of his numbed right hand.

He crouched there a moment, head canted and listening. Then, straightening, with a malicious grin he deliberately cascaded the stacked pile of currency onto the floor.

In a rage Bender struck him across the face with his pistol; but with that sound of pounding feet on the stairs he dared waste no more time. Snatching up what he could he jerked open the window—there was no chance now of going back through the hall. Throwing a leg over the sill he stuffed the recovered bills into a pocket, thrust the pistol in leather and, bringing up the other leg, twisted over on his stomach.

Outside now, gripping the sill with only the tips of his fingers, he heard Lasham yell and bitterly let himself go.

There wasn't over a twelve-foot drop beneath his feet but the alley was littered with old cans and bottles. He struck hard and went over, landing flat on his back, and the force of the impact knocked all the breath out of him. Black shapes filled the window and his picture of these was laced with bright flashes and the sound of the guns was like hell with the hatch off.

Bender sprang to his feet with lead thudding all around him. He reached for his gun, thinking to drive them from the window, but the fall must have jarred it out of his holster. He took to his heels like an old cow in fly time, knowing they'd be after him now in grim earnest.

He got to the tamarisk barely in time to see Chucho, reins flying, make off into blackness.

Bender didn't have enough breath left to curse with. He saved what he had to keep himself going and plowed on through the trash with his heart pounding wildly. He had wrenched his left leg in that drop from the window and before he had reached the third building he was staggering. He had to reach a horse soon or concede he was done for; he hadn't a chance to elude a thorough search in this town and only along the lighted portions of the street would he be at all likely to get hold of a horse.

He cut down the next alley, each breath a raw agony, each new fall of his weight on that left foot sending splinters of pain jabbing through him like fire. Somehow he kept going. He came into the street, saw a tierack of horses hitched before a saloon, eyes guiding him unerringly to the best of the lot, a hammer-headed roan that had a lot of bottom to him.

He could still hear the uproar—even through the in-and-out wheeze of his breathing he could hear Lasham yelling like a prodded steer. He jerked loose the roan's reins and got a foot in the stirrup. When his hand touched the horn the damned bronc started pitching but he got aboard him anyway and wheeled him into the street. The horse got his head down, started bucking in earnest. In the midst of these gyrations Bender felt the horse wilt. He thought the hammer-headed fool was trying to fold up under him until he saw the blood spurting from the hole in its neck.

That was when he heard the rifle.

He drove in his gut hooks, felt the roan rock forward, but he knew in three strides the bronc was going to die under him and kicked his feet out of the oxbows, figuring to jump. The roan folded too quick and he went over its head.

Bender tried to land rolling but he took the full impact on the backs of his shoulders. Then his weight ground one side of his face in the dirt; his legs came down like the stick from the rocket and he caught at a sort of fuddled impression of having been over this same road before.

Dimly he heard the crazed brutes get under way, the clacking of horns, the shouting and swearing, the futile popping of cork-stopper guns as the hard-spurring hands made desperate efforts to head them. They couldn't do it, of course. He would like to have brained the fool who'd flapped that blanket. What a thunder they made as with increased tempo the wild run of those hoofs avalanched ever nearer. Like the roar of an express train crossing a trestle—and the dust! He could feel the grit of it under his teeth, the scorched stench of it seeping through the folds of his bandanna. In a kind of a panic he pushed himself over, got his head up a little and saw where he was.

He would have taken the stampede if he'd had any choice. His fall had thrown him within ten feet of the horse and tiny snakes' heads of dust were spurting up all about him, and it didn't seem possible with so much lead being thrown they hadn't shot him into doll rags.

He didn't wait for them to do it. With the front of that howling mob still twenty yards from being on top of him he rolled frantically for cover. He brought up behind the slaughtered horse and, dragging the Winchester off the saddle, he levered three slugs into the front of that bunch and saw them break like startled quail. He knocked one skinny guy flat on his kisser. Sent another doubling over like he'd caught a dose of colic. Three brace of horses at a hitchrack tore the top rail loose and went through the scattering crowd like a scythe through standing sorghum.

Bender didn't wait to see what else might happen. There were three nags still nervously fretting and pawing before the lighted windows of a place on the corner whose fresh-painted sign read TIGER LILY BAR—Jas. Bascomb, Prop.; and he stumbled to his feet, weaving drunkenly over the pot holes, desperately striving to reach those horses before they bolted.

He saw the largest go down like a poleaxed steer while he yet hadn't covered more than half the distance. Cursing, he whirled, savagely emptying the rifle, seeing one man come staggering out of a grog shop's doorway.

He let go of the useless saddle gun, shambling into a wheezing run, his wrenched leg commencing to act up again. He watched the whole middle drop out of a window—saw the place go black as those inside snuffed the lamps.

He still had a couple dozen strides to go and had just about decided which of the remaining pair he'd take when the horse of his choice went screaming up on hind legs and, with forefeet thrashing madly, fell thin-squealing over on its back. The unhit horse shied the length of its reins, snorting with terror, its eyes rolling crazily as gun-thrown lead kicked splinters off the tierail.

With a groan of despair Bender dived at the animal, was inches short of getting a hand on its cheekstrap when the soaped reins parted. The gelding's braced weight flung it back on its haunches and, before it could whirl, Bender's hand was in its mane. The frightened horse whirled anyway but Bender got one knee around the pommel and, as the bay broke into a headlong run, he clutched both arms around its neck and clung there.

The horse careened dizzily around the Tiger Lily's far corner, gathering fresh momentum with every stride it took. The guns were lost in the scream of the wind and not until the last of the lights were left behind did Bender pull himself into the saddle.

13 | THE BUSTED FLUSH

THE horse, plunging forward, had its nose pointed east and for a long five minutes after quitting the town Bender permitted it to run before reducing its speed to an easier lope designed to keep a few beans in the boiler. There was no sense at all in fooling himself; what had happened in that room had changed all the values and they would not now be saving him for anything. They'd prefer him dead, and the deader the better.

He wheeled the bay off the road, thankful there would be no moon for at least another hour. They wouldn't bother for a while with trying to pick up his tracks; they'd expect him to head south with that money and, if he went that way, they'd have him bottled between themselves and the sheriff's posse. For him to keep going east would be almost as bad for if they failed to turn him up this side of the Floridas they would guess right away that he had lined out for Crater intending to by-pass the mountains and drop south from there. Not until they still failed to find him would it occur to them he might have gotten cold feet and be trying to get out of the country. When they reached this thought they would head back to town for a look at his tracks. By then it ought to be daylight.

This should give him five hours, maybe six if he were lucky. In that length of time, swinging north to further confuse them and then bearing west to make trailing harder through the hills below Holy Cross, he should be entering

Columbus. From Columbus to Tres Pinos on a good fresh horse hadn't ought to take longer than another three hours.

Scanning these conclusions for faulty reasoning and not finding any beyond the natural complexities of human behavior, Bender pointed the gelding's nose into the north and let him break briefly into a gallop.

He wasn't underestimating Lasham. He knew very well if he fell into the sheep king's hands before morning he would be a cooked goose and no two ways about it.

The man would never feel safe so long as Bender was at large with that confession in his pocket, but by morning the sheep king's mind should be working with all its normal cunning. He would realize then he had to go at this careful. That confession in the wrong hands could get Deef Lasham lynched, and he had made too many enemies to relish taking needless chances. He wouldn't be throwing any honest law at Bender; he would send picked men that he could trust to keep their mouths shut.

But anyway, regardless of what Lasham did or did not do, Bender couldn't sidestep the knowledge that Tres Pinos had first call on him. Don Leo needed the money in Bender's pockets and there was Blanca to be thought of. Disquieting as he had found the girl—he was sure he didn't like one thing about her, including that carnal appeal to the senses—there was always the chance that Lasham, misinterpreting what she had done at the jail, would seek to reach Bender through striking at her.

Sand hummocks were lifting their gray shapes around him when he turned the horse west and pulled it down to a walk. He wasn't too happy about the gelding's action; it was much too inclined to shows of impatience to have any large amount of stamina, he thought. But he was stuck with it now and until he could get another he would have to conserve all he could of its strength.

He got to wondering how much of that money he'd come off with, and from this speculation his mind turned to Red Hat. At least he wouldn't have to be worrying about Hazel. That shattered elbow he had given the sheep boss would keep

Syd Hazel pretty well under wraps and, with him out of the
running, Bender reckoned he could make it pretty goddam
costly for anyone who tried to cross Tres Pinos with Lasham's
sheep.

It was a comforting thought but it didn't last longer than
a June frost in Texas. He was suddenly remembering that
swift scratching of the pen as Hazel signed Deef Lasham's
confession. It had been a natural thing, instinctive and without trouble, for the burly sheep boss to scrawl his name
left-handed.

Bender cursed with a whole-hearted bitterness. The man
was a southpaw! Instead of putting Syd Hazel on the sidelines
for keeps that busted right arm was like to get Bender's neck
broke. Nothing loomed surer than that Red Hat wouldn't rest
until he'd evened the score plumb complete with compound
interest.

FAR to the southeast the lights of Deming still showed
faintly when Bender, anxious to get into the hills, finally
turned the bay south. By this time, near as he was able to
figure, Lasham's crew of drunks and barflies should have met
up with Fentress' posse, discovered the fugitive hadn't cut
south, and be lining out for Crater.

The terrain commenced to get more broken up. The grease-
wood thinned, there was a lot more yucca and the grass came
in tufts, poking out of the drifts like fringe round the sides of
a bald man's skull. For the last three-four miles he'd been
traveling in cycles; walk awhile, jog awhile, strike a high gallop. They were in the walk now with the ground rising under
them and everything someway seeming plainer than before.
Abruptly jerking up his head Bender found suspicion verified.
Beyond a black peak less than five miles distant, round and
orange and very large, the moon was making its appearance.

He came out of his thinking, hauling the bay up sharply,
with a faint impression of dust in his nostrils. For an uncon-
scionable time he sat motionless, listening, but unable to
catch any rumor of riders; and finally, snorting disgustedly,
he relaxed his grip, the gelding resuming its head-nodding ad-

vance. *Getting jumpy,* Bender thought, not liking the notion.

A hundred yards later the bay dropped into a wash. This was a broad one, deep sided, more than sixty feet across with a thick growth of brush along the west rim where its course swung east around a ledge of uncovered sandstone. It was darker down here, the dry bottom glimmering with its myriad of mica.

Half way across this floor he smelled dust again and, this time, there wasn't any doubt of it. Riders had passed this way within minutes and a couple strides later he came onto their tracks. They were heading upstream, going south and going without sign of any obvious hurry. If they'd been traveling in the open he would have written them off for punchers ranchward bound from an evening in Holy Cross. As it was, they might be rustlers on their way to lift somebody's cattle.

With lips squeezed together he put the bay into motion, urging the animal toward the opposite bank.

He was on the way up when he heard them coming. One moment the wash loomed completely empty, in the next three riders suddenly bulged into sight.

Bender kept the bay climbing, looking over his shoulder. It didn't take those fellows very long to spot him. The one in the center yelled: "That you, Sim?"

Bender, not stopping, threw a grunt back for answer and the man called irritably, "Where the hell is that barber?"

Not risking an answer Bender flung a hand northward, but just as the bay got into the brush one of the men down below snarled, "That ain't Sim!" and Bender kicked in the hooks.

He heard the thin whine, the double crash of two rifles, and flung himself forward to get his shape off the skyline. He heard yells on both sides and before he could swerve, the bay with the bit in its teeth was rocketing full tilt into a group of stopped horsebackers.

Bender heard a scared curse. He saw the pale shrinking blobs of startled uptilted faces and kicked both booted feet free of the stirrups. The bunch tried to scatter but he was too soon into them, the bay careening headlong into a red dun's middle. Bender left its back in a flying tackle. One out-flung arm wrapped round a beard-framed face and, like blown chaff, this man was swept from the saddle. He commenced a frightened squawk but the ground thumped it out of him. Bender rolled clear, the squawker's gun in one fist, the squawker's reins in the other.

He triggered three shots into that milling confusion; through the shouts and yells he drove one more and watched a man spill backward off the rump of a rearing pinto. Flinging himself into the captured gray's saddle, Bender emptied the pistol and spurred into the brush.

This was the same stretch of brush he had so recently come out of, the brush that concealed the west rim's ragged lip. Breathing hard, Bender braced both feet in the stirrups and pulled the horse to a stop with its still skidding hoofs barely inches from the brink. In one blurred motion he was out of the saddle. In the next he had the stallion turned completely around and, crouching low, reached up and got a grip on its nostrils. The horse tried to shake loose but, using his grip like a twitch, Bender forced the big brute into a stance of utter quiet.

There wasn't one chance in ten this play could have fooled any man who had his wits about him. Bender was staking his life on the belief this bunch was too muddle-minded to know straight up from down—and he was right.

A guy with a bull-throated voice was bellowing, "After him, you pinheaded nitwits!"

"Where the hell did he go?"

"He went down in that wash—"

"Not while we was there," the one who'd yelled at Sim said. "We just come outa that wash an'—"

"That's when he done it. Just as you was comin' up. I seen his hat drop outa sight off't the right of that stunted cedar."

"Yeah," another voice backed this one up. "He was on Treeny's gray an' he was sure as hell headin' south—"

"He was headed *north!* He turned on the lip; I seen his shoulders comin' round—"

"You goddam fools," shouted Bull Throat, "git down there after him 'fore we lose him!"

"I don't see *you* bustin' your pants out t' git there!"

"What's Fentress want him for, anyway?" asked another; but nobody answered him.

Bull Throat said, "Dave you take three of these boys an' cut north up that wash. You take the other pair, Curly, an' cut south."

"An' what'll *you* be doin', Mister Godlemighty Jones?"

"I'll stay right where I'm at in case he tries to double back."

"That's a damn thoughty notion," one of the others pronounced approvingly. "Mebbe I better stay with you. Just in case you ain't able to stop him."

"Hell—come on," some one else growled disgustedly. "That feller's prob'ly halfway to Mexico by this time—or Canada."

Bender heard horses moving, the creak of leather, the tinkle of spur chains. Treeny's gray was getting tired of this and so, for that matter, was Bender's hand, not to mention the rest of his still-crouched anatomy. Time, that so precious commodity, was passing and the moon, cheese yellow, was getting higher and brighter.

Now the sound of breaking brush lifted two diverging lines of clatter. Bender longed, so covered, to let go of the stallion and reload Treeny's pistol but he knew, if he did, the damned horse would betray him.

There was the cold feel of sweat along the back of his neck and a mounting rage was burning away the controls of his caution as it became increasingly evident his inspired ingenuity was about to leave him in a first class jackpot.

Had he kept on going when he'd first wrapped his legs about the quivering gray he would have gotten clean away from this procrastinating outfit. Trying to play it smart had handicapped him intolerably and in another few moments they'd have him glued to this brush like a fly to gummed paper. Already that moon was too bright for his liking and if he clung to this place much longer and these birds ever got spread out on three sides of him . . .

He brought his back out of its cramp a little, minded to run for it while he still had a chance. Neither part of the split posse had yet got quite abreast of him and, with surprise in his favor, he could probably get into the wash. He had a terrible urge to make the try and only his remembrance of the thing restrained him. Common sense told him he could never get across sixty feet of deep sand fast enough to beat the bullets this pack would be sending after him.

He tightened his hold on the gray while he listened to the sound of the southmost group file past. While its noise was still close, their horses slithering down the bank, he pulled the stallion deeper into the concealment of dusty foliage, his idea being to get away from the edge where there was now too much chance of the horse being spotted by the men who'd just passed him.

He made the shift without discovery but the dust shaking down off the bushes almost strangled him. He had to fight for every breath and, to aggravate him further, the horse started pawing up a fresh cloud off the ground. Bender had to lean against the gray to keep it enough off balance to stop this.

"Hey, Treeny!" came an E-string whine from the wash. "That guy never come down here. Only tracks we kin find's our own. Outside of the ones he left goin' over."

"Hell, we seen him. Look again."

"We already hev."

"Then hunt his sign along the bank."

"We done that, too. I tell you that ranny's pulled a fast one someway. If you're wantin' *my* notion he never come outa that brush."

The dust got the best of him and Walt Bender sneezed.

14 | "START MAKIN' TRACKS!"

BENDER froze against the horse as stiff as any startled posseman, hardly daring even to breathe in the intensified ear-ringing silence. He felt like something chained in a vacuum until the fed-up gray tried to kick him. In his angered excitement Bender gave the brute too hard a shove and the off-balance horse fell into the brush like a wagonload of bricks dumped against a tin siding.

For an outraged instant Bender hung on the edge of braining the beast; then he heard Treeny's yell and shouts from the wash intermingled with hoofbeats tore through the petrified chaos of his emotions and, with a snarled curse, Bender sheathed the emptied pistol. He kicked the horse to his feet, slammed into the saddle and raked the gray's sides with the spiked wheels of his spurs.

The stallion took off like something hurled from a catapult. A pair of rifles cracked viciously from Treeny's position, flame licking pallidly across the bright moonlight, and then the big gray was out in the open, streaking south like the haze funneled up in a twister. He struck another patch of brush and ripped his way through it like a mill saw going through a twenty-foot plank. He had speed to burn and Bender used it, the sounds of the posse falling rapidly away in a fading whisper that was soon gone entirely, swallowed up in the night.

He was five miles into the tumbled hills when Bender caught the first rumor of another rider. The gray had latched onto its second wind and was running smoothly through the blues and silvers of the shadow-dappled range. Ahead in the distance, perhaps four hundred yards, there was a black

stand of pine darkening the brow of a ridge, and Bender sent
the gray toward this without slackening its gait.

They went into these fast, then Bender's knees slowed the
horse and swung it left at right angles, holding it down to a
lope as they paralleled the ridge just inside the belt of trees.
In this direction the pines extended their cover a quarter mile
and, just before they hit the open, Bender pulled the stallion
up. He could hear the other's hoofbeats coming on at a pushing pace, reaching down from the north over ground the gray
had covered.

He sat quiet, grimly listening, knowing his own dust wake
must be guiding this unseen rider. Unquestionably this fellow
was one of that left-behind posse, a man with a mount fully
as good as his own; and with his lips pulled back off his teeth
Bender lifted the Winchester from beneath his stirrup fender.

He got down and, tying the gray, sank onto a knee where
he could watch the bright ridgeside and, almost at once, he
saw the rider streak out of a fold in the hills and pound
toward the place where he'd come into the trees.

Too far for good rifle range. Bender, knowing this, lowered
the Winchester and got to his feet. No sense in warning him.
Better to let him go and ride his wake or, better still, cut
farther east and thus avoid any chance of an ambush. Any
man who could track another by smell would be too canny
to go far after losing the scent.

Then, just as he was about to go back to the gray, Bender
saw the rider, now partway up the slope, pull his horse to a
stop and twist his head this way and that. He looked like a
puzzled dog sniffing air and, sure enough, after a moment
he started cutting for sign. You could tell when he found it
by the sharp way he stopped and sat there studying the trees.

This guy was too smart to have been with that posse.
Bender's dodge in the brush wouldn't have fooled him a moment. Bender hadn't any notion of who he was, nor did he
give a damn. This bird was too slick to do any messing
around with.

He watched the man ease his horse into motion again,
abruptly turn it east in a track paralleling the line of trees.

The fellow was too wary to come into these pines; he was going to skirt their edges and cut Bender's sign beyond them. If
Bender let him.

Bender had no intention of letting him. Estimating by present progress the point at which horse and rider would pass
nearest and, allowing for elevation, Bender again raised the
rifle and, with narrowed eyes, waited. A hundred yards was
duck soup with a saddle gun but, just as the man was about to
ride into Bender's sights, something frightened him. He yanked
the dun's head around, spurring him savagely. Bender knocked
the horse sprawling before he'd taken three jumps.

He rode into Columbus an hour after sunrise.

He took the big gray to a livery. He turned him over to the
hostler with explicit instructions concerning bed and board.
They went out and looked over what the guy had for sale,
Bender finally parting with forty dollars for a mouse-colored
gelding with one gotched ear. The animal had no real claim
to beauty but at least it looked reasonably durable.

With the gray's gear hung up and with a secondhand
rig on Don Quixote, Bender moved into the shine of the sun.
He racked at a hash house where he treated himself to ham,
eggs and coffee, battening this down with two slabs of apple
pie. After which he once again climbed aboard his mouse-
colored hack and struck out for the West Potrillos.

The trip took four hours of damned weary riding.

He knew as soon as he sighted the house he wasn't going
to be getting any sleep just yet. A strange horse was standing
on dropped reins by the gallery and, at the far end of it, a
number of *peones* with their straw hats in their hands were
staring open-mouthed at a gesticulating *gringo* who appeared
to think shouting was the key to translation. He didn't look
to be making much headway but with a contemptuous flap
of the hands he dismissed them, gave his gun belt a hitch,
and went into the house.

Bender had no need to catch the flash of his shirt-front to
know he had been looking at Cash Fentress, the sheriff. He

had recognized the man about as soon as he had seen him. He let the *grulla* stop and sat awhile considering. Fentress obviously hadn't seen him. He could still back away and hang around out of sight until Lasham's bought law had departed.

He could, but he knew mighty well that he wouldn't for he never had been able to convince himself there was any real profit in postponing the inevitable.

Arrived at the gallery he stepped off his horse. Inside he could hear Fentress laying the law down. By his tell of it Don Leo was not only consorting with criminals but had actually gone so far as deliberately to employ one.

If the old man was in there he was keeping his mouth shut, something few Texans would have had the wit to do.

"Furthermore," Fentress snarled, "so long as there's a plaster on this haywire outfit, I don't wanta hear of you sellin' off any of them cattle—savvy? You tell them tamale-eatin' never-sweats of yourn to scatter that herd an' *leave* it scattered!"

Bender loosened the reloaded pistol in his holster, quietly crossed the gallery and stepped through the open door.

He saw the girl's lifted chin. He saw her father's frozen features and, over across the room, he saw the Three Pines ramrod intently engrossing himself with a hangnail.

Blanca was saying stiffly: "What we do with our cattle can be no concern of yours."

"I can damn well make it my concern," the sheriff snapped. Then his tone simmered down and a kind of leer crept into it. "I reckon you'd find me reasonable if you'd exert yourself a little."

Don Leo got angrily out of his chair but Blanca said with a deal of composure, "I suppose you mean if I would go to bed with you."

"Well, I wasn't figurin' to put it that plain—"

"You don't need to. I won't. I wouldn't wipe my feet on a *gringo* whore's son who would use his badge to steal a girl's virginity."

The sheriff's neck turned red. "You'll come beggin' for the chance to be nice to me, sister, before I git done with this damn greaser outfit! I ain't forgot you busted that crook outa jail an' for two cents, by Gawd, I'd—"

The sheriff's wind whistled out, his wide-eyed stare gone incredulously down to the pair of bright pennies which had just struck the floor within inches of his boots. These had come from behind him and Fentress, blanching, settled into his tracks like a squatting duck.

The girl's scathing laugh fetched his rage back, cheeks livid, spun him round like a cat and sent his hand slapping hipward. His muscles jammed, locked solid, as the spread fingers curled about the handle of his pistol, clamped there immovable, frozen by the fear of what he read in Bender's gaze.

"Don't drag that iron unless you're figurin' to use it!"

The sheriff stood rock still while the visible strain dug gaunter lines beneath his cheekbones. Some bitter thought laid its murderous track across the stare that couldn't quite conceal the sheriff's frightened indecision and, resorting to bluster, he caught his breath in a snarl. "You're under arrest! Hear me? Git your goddam hands up!"

"For what?" Bender said.

"For assault, for battery, for armed robbery and coercion, forced entry, breakin' jail, disturbin' the peace an' for the willful abduction of Jake Paintor's bay geldin'—"

Bender laughed in his face.

"You better come," the lawman spluttered. "You better not make your case no worse than it is. You got the best of me by a trick but don't think tricks'll git you out of this. There's a bunch of hard-ridin' posses combin' the brush for you right now an' if you ever expect to git to trial you better come with me an' you better come peaceful. I'll do what I—"

"Come up for air," Bender said derisively.

"There's a law in this land!" Fentress shouted; and Bender's eyes turned black with hate. He caught the sheriff by the slack of his shirt and hauled him forward with a savage tug, tripping him over an out-thrust boot. When the squawking putty-faced lawman stumbled Bender fastened a second savage hold on his belt and, carrying him that way, stepped through the door and heaved him into the hoof-tracked dust.

"Three Pines don't need your kind of law. If you ever show up on this ranch again I'll make it my business to see you're planted here permanent. Now get onto your hind legs and start makin' tracks!"

15 | POINT AND COUNTERPOINT

BENDER, rubbing his palms on the legs of his levis, came into the room and pinned a hard glance on the face of Gonzales.

"There's only one way to handle skunks, Pedrocito."

The foreman's look turned sullen with hatred. He got out of his chair with a desperate lunge when he saw the big Texan commence to start toward him. One fist dived into his sash and got hung there when Bender's iron grip flung him into the wall. "Is this the way you watch out for those cattle?"

He shoved the man roughly in the direction of the doorway, anger deepening the angles of his cheeks, eyes winter bright with an unforgiving fury. "When you ran this spread you did as you pleased. *I'm* running it now and you'll do what I say or I'll break every bone in your white-livered carcass. Now get out on that range and stay with that stock till you've got a buyer's check in your pocket—go on! Clear out of here now before I lose my temper."

There was no talk in the room until Gonzales' steps faded. The old man sat wrapped in a dismal kind of quiet and the girl's face was marble with no expression on it.

Then her head came around. Her glance locked with Bender's and he could read in her eyes the veiled disgust and suspicion his proximity seemed always to arouse in her. From the very first, even when she'd been working hardest to enlist his aid in behalf of Tres Pinos, antagonism had been the keynote of their relations. Flint against steel.

Bender's mouth corners tightened.

"I approved," she said, "the way you handled Cash Fentress, but you didn't waste very much thought on Gonzales—"

"He got all he had coming."

"That's a sample of your attitude. The ranch should come first no matter what you think of him—"

"I put the ranch first."

"You took a poor way of showing it. The man was following your orders. He put two men at the shack, he put the rest with the cattle. He rode in this morning to see about that poison—"

"Nobody asked him to see about that poison!"

They glared at each other, hate in both their faces. Blanca drew in her breath and let it out again carefully. "The man represents a vital portion of our resources—surely you can see that? With a little more tact you might have managed to retain his tolerance. Now he'll hate you—"

"I can stand it," Bender said.

"But the point you seem to have overlooked completely is that this hatred for you may undermine his whole outlook. His loyalty."

"That would be too bad—for Pete," Bender grunted. The heat of his anger still rode through his glance and the rage smouldering in him stared uncaringly out of it. "You hired me to save this ranch from Lasham's sheep. If you'll keep out of my hair long enough I may do it."

"I'm not sure," Blanca said, "that I care for your methods."

"They at least have the merit of getting results." He dug the roll of bills out of his pocket, clanked across the room and dropped it into Don Leo's lap. "Count out your forty-five hundred. If there's anything over it belongs to me."

The old man stared at the bills he was holding. It seemed to take a long time for their significance to reach him. Bender saw incredulous hope break through the gray mask of the rancher's indifference. His jaw started quivering. When he finally commenced to thumb through them he had to stop twice to still the shaking of his hands.

Bender grinned, feeling good, and went back to face Blanca, not expecting any thanks but certainly not prepared for the smile of cold scorn which flattened the lips across her teeth.

"Only an optimist, I suppose," she said, "could have expected anything different from a gun-hung drifter picked up off the desert."

"What's the matter?" he scowled. "I got what I went after —I got your dough back, didn't I?"

"But those lease lands are gone—of what good is this money? You stupid fool!" she cried bitterly. "Why didn't you fetch back the note we gave for it?"

A FAR piece of Bender's mind heard the old man get up and move across to the table. "Fifty-three hundred eighty dollars," he chuckled. *"Dinero mucho.* The Blessed Virgin be praised. There will be no need to dispose of my cattle, no need to put that accursed poison . . . eh?"

Bender could feel Don Leo's puzzled stare, could sense the rancher's shrug. *"No le hace—*I will leave your money on this table, *amigo."*

The old man's boots tapped their heels toward the patio. Bender looked at Blanca while the stillness piled up and got quieter than silence and his thoughts tramped around the inescapable truth.

She was right. He had been seven kinds of a nitwitted nump to go risking his neck getting hold of that money when he might just as easily have demanded the note. He'd been ramming around like a chicken with its head off, and to about as much purpose. He'd got the money all right but, so far as the girl was concerned, all he had accomplished was to cut the cards back to where they'd been in the first place. A hell's smear of motion but no tangible results. Lasham still had the note. Tres Pinos was still mortgaged.

"When's that borrowed money due?"

"On the tenth. Twelve o'clock noon."

Seven days. One week. Around a hundred and sixty hours.

more or less. Bender scowled at his knuckles. With the money
on hand that seemed like plenty of time to get the slate rubbed
clean. And ordinarily it would be. Only he knew damned well
they'd never get that note paid off so long as Lasham could
prevent it. He would move heaven and earth to keep that note
unpaid and, if it didn't get paid, he was going to move in here
come hell or high water. A couple of hundred dead sheep
weren't going to hold him back.

Blanca said with her eyes still hating him, "What have you
got in mind to do next?—if I'm permitted to share your confidence."

"We've got to have more men."

"You've got thirteen now—"

"You can't run this ranch, move those cattle, hold off the
sheep and get that money to Lasham with thirteen men! Out of
the question."

"You'll be able to. Just put that magnificent brain to
work—"

Bender scowled angrily. "If we're to save this spread we've
got to all pull together—"

"You should have thought of that when you were bullying
Pete."

All the unnatural restraints which Bender had been forci-
bly imposing on himself commenced to tear loose in a rush of
fury. He caught hold of her wrist and they glared at each
other in a fast-breathing silence. Cheeks white, she struggled
to break his hold and, goaded anew by the look on her face,
he took a perverse delight in piling on pressure until she suddenly cried out and then, ashamed, he let her go.

She got back away from him, rubbing her wrist, her eyes
looking wild as a cougar's. "If you ever try that again I will
kill you."

"Yeah? With kindness, I reckon!" Bender laughed without
humor and strode into the patio.

Don Leo stood by the barrel with a little jar of insects he
had captured among the shrubs. As Bender came up he could
hear the old man clucking. Even a kid in three-cornered pants,
he thought angrily, would have better judgment than to coddle

a goddam snake—particularly one for whose bite there was no known antidote.

He said without preamble: "We've got to have more men. You know where I can get them?"

"*Los bravos?*"

"Men who know how to use a gun anyway. This is going to get rough and—"

"There are such men in Deming but with what would we pay them? All the money I have is that which you just gave me."

Bender chewed at his lip.

"What is it that you have in your mind, *amigo?* Perhaps my good friend Cuerna Vaca, at Tularosa—"

Bender shook his head. "We can't wait that long. What about these *peones*, these *mozos* you've got lollin' around?"

Don Leo smiled sadly. "They are as children, *senor*—"

"They can pull a trigger, can't they?"

"What would you wish them to do?"

"We've got to finish that roundup, get the herd off to market. You've got just seven days to pay off that note; we've got to spread that poison and we've got to have men ready to stand off those sheep—"

"But what need have we now to dispose of my cattle? Surely—"

"*Need!*" Bender shouted. "My God, Leo, do you honestly believe that wool-lovin' vinegarroon is going to throw in his hand just because we've got that money back? He'll hit you with everything he can get hold of!"

"But the cattle . . . I don't see—"

"Look," Bender growled. "He's comin' up from the desert. The only way he can get into Tres Pinos is by the trail that comes up past that shack on the bluffs, so between here and there is where we dump that poison. You don't want your cattle eatin' strychnine, do you?

"Now, to give him a legal excuse to go through here, he's got to be able to show he owns a chunk of this outfit; that's why he made you that loan on a short-term note an' got you to put up this spread for security. He's goin' to try to go

through anyway, but if you pay off the note he won't have
the courts back of him. Obviously then he's going to do all
he can to make sure you can't pay it. One thing he can do
is keep out of your way. While you're rampin' around with
that money tryin' to find him you'll be a first-class target for
robbery, won't you? Same way with those cattle—they repre-
sent a cash asset. Try to keep them here and he'll set Chesseldine onto 'em; try movin' them out an' Chesseldine's gang
will make a play to stampede them. To fight that bunch off,
whether we hold them here or move 'em, we're going to need
every damn one of your cowboys. While they're engaged with
the cattle Lasham brings in the sheep. Now do you see why we
need more men?"

Time's furrows showed plainly in Don Leo's cheeks. He
stared haggardly at Bender. "We have no chance at all?"

"We've got a chance, a mighty slim one. But I've got to
have more men. We've got to use these *mozos;* I'd like to hire
a few leather slappers—the hell of it is we haven't got much
time."

They stared at each other. The old man said with touching
faith, "I put myself in your hands. Tell me what I can do."

"You can organize these *mozos.* Give every man a rifle. Put
a couple of them to work with a wagon shovelin' strychnine.
Take the rest of them down to that shack on the bluffs and
make a big show of guardin' that trail. You better stay right
with them; that way, maybe, they won't break and run before
we're ready to take over with our big artillery. Once Lasham
understands you're intending to use force he'll probably sit
tight until that note falls due. This much I'm sure of—his
Yaquis won't move without he gives them the nod."

He was about to set off for the stables, intending if he
could to catch Gonzales before he left and revise his instructions with regard to the roundup, when the old man hesitantly
reached out a hand. "What do you think I should do about
that money?"

Bender swung around. His eyes looked worried, undecided.
"That's as tough a nut as we've got to crack. Anything you
try is going to be damn risky." He glowered at the knuckles

of his left hand a moment. "Tell you what," he said finally—
"if you want to trust me to take care of it I'll see what I
can do."

Don Leo, obviously happier, thrust the money into his hand.

Bender stuffed it carelessly into a pocket. "You camp out
on that bluff until you see me again."

HE went back through the house, caught up the reins of
his *grulla* and got into the saddle. About to line out for the
scene of the roundup he decided, inasmuch as he could not
hire any men short of one of the towns, to catch up a fresh
mount and turned, instead, toward the stables.

Going around the huge house he turned Don Quixote toward the gate which led into the *parada*. Engrossed with his
problems he'd put the gelding through the gate before the
sound of the girl's voice fully jerked him out of his thinking.
A saddled horse on dropped reins dozed not ten feet in front
of him and beyond its sorrel bulk Blanca was talking to
Gonzales who had not, it would seem, been in any great sweat
to get back to the cattle.

Bender's knees involuntarily put a brake on the *grulla*, but
he would have gone on immediately to apprise the foreman of
his latest intentions had the girl not said, "But that's silly—
you should know me better than to believe anything so stupid.
You *can't* quit us now!"

"I will not work for this pig of a *gringo*," Gonzales said
furiously. "Do you think I have no pride at all?"

"Would you let your pride—"

"It is not only that! I have seen the way you look at this
fellow—"

"Tres Pinos needs his gun and his experience. He knows
these people as we could never hope to know them; he has a
feud with this Lasham—"

"Do not tell me these lies. They have nothing to do with
the way you look at him. *Sangre de Cristo*—do you think I
am a fool?"

"You are beginning to convince me," she said coldly. Then,

softening: "How can you be so blind, Pedrocito? For this man I care nothing—"

"Is that why you let him put his mouth on your mouth?"

"Are you now to become my *duenna* also?"

"*Por Dios,* you need one," Gonzales growled huskily. Gravel grated harshly beneath the twist of a boot. Their shadows merged, clung and broke apart.

"There," she said with a breathless laugh. "Can you believe me now? Ah, *pobrecito,* do not look so fierce. That Yankee gossoon is but a means to an end, a thing to be used, fire against fire for the good of the *rancho*—"

"*Querida* . . . I love you so much I could kill you . . ."

Tight-lipped, Bender kneed his horse forward. Swinging into their orbit he got out of the saddle, tossed his reins at the girl and said to Gonzales, "How long will it take you to get the herd ready?"

Gonzales' eyes were suspicious. He growled sullenly in Spanish, "Perhaps three more days."

"Make it two. Add three more for the road and you should have it in Columbus this side of nightfall Thursday—"

"Columbus! I thought you meant to sell it in Deming—"

"Those plans have been changed. You'll take it to Columbus and keep your eyes skinned every step of the way. You'll have trouble with Chesseldine so, to make sure you get through, you will take the whole crew—"

"Then what of the ranch? What about those sheep?"

"We'll worry about that when they get here. Your job's the cattle. You have them in Columbus before the sun sets Thursday. I'll have a buyer waiting to take delivery at the stock yards."

AFTER the foreman had gone Blanca, realizing she held Bender's reins, threw them down. Her eyes looked as though she were going to curse him. "I'm not your *moza,*" she said on an indignant outrush of breath. "I understood from the first you were a mannerless barbarian, but I did not think you would stoop to plain spying."

Bender's ears grew hot under her scornful regard and the

knowledge that he was flushing was fresh fuel to his anger. "At least a Yankee gossoon would have more regard for the conventions than to let a half-breed paw—"

She struck him across the face, her eyes blazing.

Bender sneered. "I'm surprised, being a spik, you didn't go for a knife."

She said with biting contempt: "No matter how low a *gringo* gets he is always able to see himself as being infinitely better than—"

"You're goddam right! Your ol' man can see it, too! Why else would he have sent you to a *gringo* school an' be all the time aping us every way he knows how? He's got more sense than you'll ever have!"

Cold scorn bared her teeth and he said, determined to hurt her, "Bet you'd never catch *him* ruttin' around in a stableyard with—"

She did have a knife after all, he discovered. With a flash of white leg she tore it out of her garter. The wicked glitter of that blade was no less savage than her look. She sprang at him in a rush that came within an ace of skewering him.

He leaped back in quick alarm but she was after him like a wildcat. She seemed everywhere at once and that damned blade was like a snake's tongue. Three times it ticked him, slicing cloth, and it was all he could do to keep his legs under him as he went reeling backward, twisting and swerving in his desperate attempts to keep himself clear.

He began to sweat. He began to wonder if he was going to outlast it, tired as he was with all those hours in the saddle. He tried to grab her wrist and lost part of a shirtsleeve. Gooseflesh traveled up his spine like prickly heat as he threw himself aside, barely avoiding the jump of that blade again.

He was fighting for breath now. His legs felt like lead, and the left one he'd wrenched in that drop from the window wasn't going to be able to take much more of this. He made a swift feint and thrust a boot out to trip her but those kill-crazy eyes of hers took her around it with the grace of a boxer and he saw the shimmering gleam of that naked steel leap straight for his throat.

Too late to dodge he flung his right arm up. Pain ripped from wrist all the way to his elbow and, when he saw that welling pattern of blood, all else blurred away in a white blaze of anger.

Blanca's eyes, grown enormous, were suddenly pools of frightened horror, but Bender never noticed. All he saw was her shape through a red fog of fury as he turned on his heel and swung into the saddle.

16 | A MERCHANT IN GUNSMOKE

THE urge to smash his fists into something was almost beyond his power of containing when Bender whirled the tired horse through the gate and lifted it into a headlong run. His thoughts were a welter of conflicting emotions with Blanca holding the top spot as a target—it was God's own mercy he hadn't knocked her damn teeth out! Bad enough at a time like this to be cursed with the pain of a twisted ligament as well as half groggy from lack of rest without having his gun arm put out of commission.

Still keeping the *grulla* to a ground-eating gallop he unknotted the scarf from about his neck, gave it a couple of left-handed shakes and awkwardly wound it about his cut arm. Probably lousy with germs but he had to do something to get the blood stopped. He pressed the arm to his side and kept riding. There was an all-gone feeling squirming around through his guts by the time he came in sight of the shack but he forgot all about it in his rage at not finding any guards on the job.

He saw a pair of hitched horses dozing back of the lean-to and found the pair of *vaqueros* squatted down on the porch engaged in some kind of Mexican card game.

Bender scattered the cards hell west and crooked. Both men jumped up, their faces ludicrous with fright. Bender grabbed one fellow and spun him clear around. Snatched up a rifle. Shoved it into his hands. "Now get down in that brush along the edge of the bluff an' do what you been told to do! As for you," he said to the other one, "get the gear off this horse and put it on the best of that pair out back."

He went into the shack, stripping off his shirt. In the frame of mind he'd been in leaving Blanca he'd forgotten his intention of getting a fresh horse, but one of these would do well enough. He went over to the sink, dippering himself a cold drink from the bucket of well water standing there. Then, very gingerly, he peeled off the stuck neckerchief and swished his arm around in the bucket. Damn water stung but it got some of the caked blood off. He poked around in a cupboard, got hold of a bottle marked *oil of salt,* twisted off the cap and liberally dosed the again-bleeding gash.

He stuck his head out the door and called in the man he'd put to work with the horses. "Cut the back out of these red flannels," he told him, and when the fellow, with sundry mutterings, had done so, he had the man rip the cloth into strips and bind his arm. Then he picked up his shirt and threw it down in disgust. "I'm goin' to have to have yours. Climb out of it," he growled.

The man's look, which had been curious, now reshaped in sullen resentment but he didn't put any of that feeling into words. Bender got into the shirt. It was a kind of tight fit but it covered that wrapped-up arm, which was the main thing. He said to the scowling *vaquero,* "Until the *patron* comes you're the boss. Keep your eyes skinned."

HE was ten miles along the rutted trail to Columbus before he encountered any sign of another horseman. He was into a canyon by that time and the afternoon sun was well along toward the west. There had once been a rough kind of wagon road through here but now the tracks were almost hidden in weeds and to the right of this lane the solid trunks of pines rose tall and straight; the cut-over left side was a tangle of scrubby brush and live oak.

He was just coming off the crest of a rise, jogging along at an easy rack, when cowbirds wheeled up out of the brush and went winging off soundless toward the shadow-draped crags that rimmed the canyon's left wall. Bender kept his shape flexible but his eyes turned sharp and he was not surprised when a rider came out of the trees and pulled up, hooking one knee about the horn of his saddle.

"Spare the makin's?" he asked when Bender got near enough.

"Swap for a match." Bender tossed him his Durham which he'd thoughtfully removed from the shirt left behind.

While the man rolled his smoke they considered each other. Tile-green eyes stared at Bender around the bulge of a nose that had once been broken and very carelessly set. His ears were large and cupped forward like shelves built on to rest the brim of his battered old hat; this hard-used appearance extending clear down to the run-over heels of his brush-clawed boots. His teeth made a shine when he licked his cigarette, but his eyes stayed on Bender even when he bent to touch a match to his smoke.

He passed back the sack along with a couple of matches, glance drifting lightly over Bender's right arm. "Any jobs floatin' round through your part of the country?"

"Depends what you mean by jobs," Bender said.

"I wasn't lookin' for hard work."

"A little gun work, maybe?"

"I wouldn't turn it down if you'd get the price fed up enough."

Bender, needing gun hands, had the notion this fellow might be champing on the bit. He wouldn't put it above Deef Lasham to have steered a stake-out at them. He looked the man over coolly. "My name's Bender—Walt Bender."

Bat Ears nodded his round face indifferently. "Yeah. I'm Butch Stroad." He licked a pale tongue across tobacco-stained teeth. "Heard you was runnin' the Three Pines outfit—matter of fact, I was on my way over there. Kinda figured you might be toppin' the market."

"You've got your rope twisted, Butch."

"I could shake out the kinks."

"Three Pines don't run to that kind of jack."

"Looks to me like neck meat or nothin'. An' like to be nothin' if they don't git a move on."

"Yeah," Bender said, trying to think where he had seen this fellow before. He wasn't sure he had but there seemed something—

"I don't like sheep, either."

Bender shook his head. "They're scrapin' the bottom."

"Two hundred would get my name on the payroll."

"Two hundred on top of what you're drawin' from Lasham?"

Stroad showed his sour grin. "You gotta take some kinda chance in this world. That two hundred only keeps me a week but, the way I got this thing doped out, that oughta be long as you'll have any use fer me."

"Got it all down pat, eh?"

"I got enough to git on with," Stroad said, looking cagey. "I was outside the warehouse when the star lugged you off. I was back of the jail when you went off with the skirt an' I was in the Aces Up when you an' Red Hat pitched the table."

"So now you want a job?"

"You oughta be in line fer all the help you kin locate."

"You got plenty of gall, I'll say that for you."

"Stock in trade. I'm a businessman, Bender. I know without askin' Lasham wouldn't pay two hundred."

"There's a limit to what a man can know and stay healthy."

"So I been told." Stroad stubbed out his smoke on the heel of a palm, showing his yellow teeth in another tough grin. "You buyin' or ain't you?"

"Got a pencil on you?"

"It's cash on the barrelhead, Jack. With a poor risk like you I can't afford to take chances—"

"You'll get an order on Don Leo, the owner of Tres Pinos."

"Collectable when?"

"When you get to the ranch. Providin' you don't make any detours or any changes in the note."

Stroad dug up a pencil, tore a page from a dog-eared notebook, and handed them over. Bender scribbled the note and gave it to him. "Until I get back you'll stay with the crew we've got out watchin' for the sheep."

17 | OVERTURE TO VIOLENCE

THOSE who weren't already eating were about to get ready to when Bender reached Columbus a couple of hours later. His arm was beginning to hurt like hell and, what was more disconcerting mentally, it was becoming a chore to move it. A fine shape to be in if he should run into trouble.

The nose bag could wait. He headed straight for the livery.

"Come after your nag?" the old hostler greeted.

"Right at this moment I'd like to find me a sawbones."

"Doc Slink's got a office up over the bank. Hurt yourself, did you?"

"Scratched my arm on some barb wire. You want to do something for me? Go over to the mercantile and get me a shirt and put this horse out of sight till I get back."

The doc was just about to go out for his supper. He clucked when he saw the look of Bender's arm. "Oil of salt," he snorted. "Well, you might have done worse." He cleansed the wound, swabbed medicine on it and was making ready to apply a heavy dressing when Bender said, "Somethin' flexible, Doc—"

"Now see here," said Slink sternly; "if you want that arm to get well you're going to have to take care of it."

Bender grinned without much mirth. "A guy that's as close

to the furniture as I am ain't going to be worried about no damn arm. What's more, I probably—wait a minute."

Bender chewed his lip, thinking. A derringer covered by two splints in bandage . . . but the doc would never go for it. "Oh, well," he growled, "go ahead. Wrap it up. But keep it as thin round the wrist as you can."

The doc's eyes narrowed. "Somebody gunning for you?"

"It could happen."

"I'd suggest, in that case, you keep under cover. This arm's in no condition for that kind of exercise."

Back at the livery the hostler handed him a parcel. "Only thing he had that looked big enough to fit you. Cost me—"

"Put it on the bill," Bender said, tearing open the paper. He pulled off the one he'd confiscated from the shack guard. "Who's buyin' cattle?"

"Your best bet's to wait till Bart Spurlock gits in—"

"I want to get shut of this herd in a hurry."

The old man's eyes widened. He took a good look around and lowered his voice. "Art Chesseldine's your man, then. Him or old Krantz. But you'd do better to—"

"Where'll I find Krantz?"

"I'll git word to him. How soon you want to sell 'em?"

"Thursday."

"I hope you know what you're doin'. That bugger'd skin a gnat for its hide an' taller."

"I'll worry about that when the time comes."

Shrugging into the blue shield-fronted shirt, Bender thrust in the tails and awkwardly buttoned it. Wool, by God! But at least the bandage didn't show; that was the main thing. He didn't need to look into any crystal ball to know what would happen if Lasham's crowd learned his arm had been crippled.

The hostler said, "I'm goin' to eat now. I'll have Krantz here before mornin'."

LEFT alone, Bender wearily climbed into the loft. He scooped out a bed in the darkest corner, pulled some hay down over him and tried after that to get himself a little rest, feeling more dragged out than he could ever remember.

But the wheels of his mind continued to churn. His wrenched leg ached. His arm throbbed distractingly, but with not enough distraction to put a brake on his thinking.

God, but he was pooped—and fed up, too. Lasham, in spite of everything, had got this deal sewed up. He'd bought the sheriff's star; he'd made some kind of pact with Chesseldine. And coming in with his sheep was that kill-hungry bunch of crazy Yaquis; Don Leo's *mozos* wouldn't last five minutes faced with those kind of *hombres*. No use kidding himself on that score, or of putting any hope in that slick-talking Stroad. If the guy was on the level he'd probably get cold feet.

There wasn't a chance in a thousand they'd ever get to pay that note off. There'd been little enough chance before Blanca'd carved him up. Now, with this crippled wing, he'd be the worst kind of fool if he went anywhere near Lasham.

The last thing he wanted was to think about Blanca. He thought about her anyway. She was still in his mind when sleep finally claimed him.

THE loft was blacker than a stove lid when Bender's jerked-open eyes became aware of somebody shaking him. "For Chrissake," came the hostler's aggravated tones—"you gonna pound your ear forever?"

Bender said with a groan, "What time is it?"

"What's time got to do with it? I got that feller waitin'."

Bender knuckled glued eyes and got to his feet. Every bone in his body felt as though it had been pounded but he followed the liveryman down the ladder. The man who stood waiting in the cobwebbed office was gaunt, stoop-shouldered and clad in scuffed range clothes with his face hid out behind a tangle of whiskers. "Understand you've got some cattle. How many, what breed and in what kind of condition?"

"Mixed herd. Longhorns. Around three thousand head. Pretty fair shape."

"And you'll have them here Thursday?"

"If the price is right. If it ain't I may swing 'em over to Cruces or go on to El Paso."

"If you was plannin' to do that you wouldn't have bothered

with me at all. I'll give you a dollar and a half a head, straight through, when they're tallied and in the yards here."

Without a word Bender wheeled and started for the door.

"Hold on," Krantz growled—"what's the matter with that?"

"I'm not offerin' you stolen cattle and I ain't takin' no rustler's price!"

Krantz's triangular eyes were like pieces of glass. "Then what the hell are you comin' to me for?"

"A quick sale," Bender said—"isn't that your specialty?"

"So now we get words!" Krantz's eyes smashed into the cringing hostler. "Did I ride thirty mile to get a mouth full of language?"

"He said he wanted to sell—"

"*Sell* is right." Bender shook his heavy shoulders together. "Make your bid or get off the pot."

"A tough guy we got." Krantz blew out his cheeks. "You got out-of-state cattle?"

"This stuff was raised right here."

"Well . . ." the man's tone turned dubious. He pawed at his whiskers. "I might go as high as maybe five dollars—"

"What'll you give for them right where they're at?"

"Where they're at I don't know—"

"They're within forty miles and held ready to trail."

In the light of the lantern Krantz looked at him carefully.

"There's something stinks about this or you wouldn't be tryin' . . ." Krantz let that trail off. Something fled through his stare and was gone and he said, "I notice you ain't put a name to the brand."

"I wasn't born yesterday. You ain't runnin' off with this herd till it's bought—"

"If it's bought on the ground I'll have to know where to find it."

"You'll know," Bender grinned, "after I've pocketed your money."

"You think," Krantz said angrily, "I pay out good money for a herd I ain't seen?"

"If you want this one you will. I'm givin' you a chance to beat the market; most the stuff in this country won't be

rounded up for sale for another four weeks. With the government leasing all these Indian lands there'll be a lot of new
contracts let out for beef. You could pay five dollars and
double your money—"

"It takes a crew to move cattle. And in country like this—"

"That won't bother you. There's nothin' whatever wrong
with this stock. It's a registered brand. You'll get a bonafide
bill of sale with the herd. Now put up or shut up. Do you
want them or don't you?"

"I'll give you four," Krantz scowled; and Bender took it.

LASHAM shoved away from the table. "That note falls due
Saturday morning at noon." His eyes slanched a look at the
scarfaced Mexican Bender had fired from the Tres Pinos
crew. "They'll try to pay it off—Don Leo or that dope of a
red-headed foreman. Your job's to see they don't get no chance
to. The forty-five hundred is yours if you stop 'em. That's
all. Beat it."

He waited till the man had shut the door behind him, listened till the steps had faded off down the street. "Your job,
Art, is to get rid of those cattle. Stampede 'em, steal 'em; I
don't care *what* you do just so you make sure they're gotten
off Tres Pinos and beyond any chance of that outfit gettin'
cash for 'em. Savvy?"

Chesseldine nodded and picked up his hat.

After he'd gone, Lasham said succinctly: "Syd, you're goin'
to loan Fentress here about three of your Yaquis—the best
shots you've got. You'll bring up the sheep and move them
onto Tres Pinos just as quick as the sheriff gets Bender arrested or, preferably, planted."

"What about that strychnine?"

"Bluff," Lasham sneered. "What cowman in his right mind's
goin' to scatter that stuff? However, Fentress here, when he
goes after Bender, can take a look around and, if the bastards
have put anything like that out, he can lug that don off to the
lockup, too. Of course, he may throw in with that murderin'
Texan—try to keep Fentress from arrestin' the man. In that
case, naturally, he'll be treated as an accomplice. In any civi-

lized society the law must be upheld and all infractions pun-
ished or you've got nothin' but anarchy. I trust," Lasham said,
fixing cold eyes on Fentress, "we've a capable man here . . . a
sheriff who knows his duty and can be depended on to do it."

Fentress looked from one to the other of them licking dry
lips.

"Got a tongue in you, don't you?"

The sheriff's cheeks took on a tinge reminiscent of Roque-
fort cheese. He gulped a couple of times but managed to get
his head nodded.

"It's not often," Lasham smiled, "that duty and inclination
are able to go so well in hand. By the time you get back they'll
have tried to pay that note off. You'll have to pick Enrico up
for whatever he's done about it but, once his mouth has been
permanently shut, it won't occur to me to ask what has happened to that money."

He let his teeth show more plainly. "I think we understand
each other. You'll be wanting to get ready for your trip now,
sheriff. Be back here ready to leave in ten minutes."

Hardly had the rasp of Fentress' boots dimmed away than
Red Hat said, scowling, "If you think, by God, I'm goin' to—"

"You'll naturally insist on going with them. I could hardly confide all the details to Fentress; and while we've got that
chiseling crook in the talking I may as well tell you we're going to have to get rid of him. We'll use his star to cover this
deal an' Scar Face; you can rub him out then an' pocket that
dinero. We may have to get rid of that rustler, too, but we
can work that out later."

"You want me to destroy that confession?"

"Just fetch it back," Lasham said. "I'll take care of de-
stroyin' it. Personal."

18 | THE LONG GUNS BARK

BLANCA, with a mist of old lace setting off the dark luster of hair held in place by a high-backed comb, stood irritably regarding the bullring posters that splashed a profusion of blues, reds and yellows across the blank side of the brown adobe which housed Deef Lasham's new office. Cream colored silk was about her shoulders and black taffeta molded her shapely hips in the dapples of lamplight crossing the street from the batwing doors and unshaded windows of the Caballo Colorado.

The calle de la Piedad off the plaza de la Virgen at this time of night was no kind of place for a girl unattended—certainly no place for the daughter of a don. She hadn't the faintest excuse for this loitering. The wagon was loaded. She could see how restive the team was becoming yet still she remained, moving into deep shadow, half frightened, excited and thoroughly determined.

She'd been ready to start for home when the mercantile closed two hours ago and had climbed to the seat, had the lines in her hands, when a chance remark had frozen her motionless. Two passing *vaqueros,* conversing about sheep, had mentioned Lasham and a *muy grande* office. Following this lead she had learned at the corner *botica* that the sheep king had indeed opened an office here and, armed with its address, she'd returned to her wagon.

In the gathering dusk she had driven past the place. One thought had led to another, more daring, and almost at once she had conceived this wild plan. Risky? Of course it was, but if she could get back that note. . . .

She'd left the wagon three doors down and walked back and slipped round to the rear of the establishment by way of the alley which ran between this building and the next, there discovering a grimed window which had not been bolted. About to push up the sash she was stopped by the sound of some inside movement. Returning to the street she had again passed the front, this time seeing light fanning out around drawn shades.

She'd come around to this side. Four men, singly, had gone into the building and, thus far, only three had come out. Two she had recognized, Enrico and Fentress, and sight of these had sent her hastening into the deepest shadows. Five minutes later she heard door sound again and impatiently listened to the departure of footsteps.

She drifted back to the corner. The lamp was still burning. She walked back to her wagon and spoke a few words to the restive team.

When she next passed the office the light was out.

She hurried around to the back and climbed in through the window.

Inside her eyes strained against the thick blackness. The smell of snuffed wick was an acrid presence; not even the tick of a clock broke the stillness. She could feel the battering pound of her heart and her breath seemed all to be hung up in her throat. She made herself go forward. With infinite care and hands outstretched she moved toward where the lamp smell was strongest until the front of her thighs came against unyielding wood. The touch of her hands discovered this was a desk, a rolltop and locked. She touched the still-warm base of the lamp on its top and only then remembered that she had no matches.

She closed her eyes and tried to think where she'd be most apt to find some; the room didn't appear quite so dark when she opened them. She could vaguely see the dim bulk of objects. Now, close by the desk, she saw a coat on a wall peg and snatched it down with feverish hands, ransacking its pockets; and her fingers uncovered three matches.

She let the coat drop and struck one, saw the gun belt

looped over the knob of a chair and the half of a knife sticking out of its sheath. This reminded her of Bender and a whole flood of memories tangled up her emotions till the flame of the match licked against her fingers.

Shocked out of her thinking she snuffed the match and, picking up the knife, moved back to the desk. The place seemed twice as dark now but she went grimly to work, occasionally pausing to lift her head and listen.

Abruptly the lock snapped back. The top slid up disclosing an untidy clutter of papers. She went through them hurriedly and then commenced sifting through the stuff in the pigeonholes, convinced before long the thing she sought was not there. She forced the drawers frantically; there was nothing resembling what she hunted in any of them. Did Lasham carry the note, in his wallet?

Where *was* it? If not in Lasham's pocket it was pretty near bound to have to be in this desk unless—and she hoped not— he had put it in the bank. She felt through the litter of papers once more and a sense of panic rushed through her and her fists clenched at the bitter injustice of a fate which could allow her to take such risk with so little reward for her enterprise.

She felt through the drawers again without finding it. A growing conviction of disaster had hold of her, warning her, urging her to get out of this place, but she wouldn't give up while there still seemed a chance she might uncover the note.

She took her chin in her hand and thought for a bit, but the most likely place was obviously this desk. She pulled the center drawer out and ran her hands along the tracks without finding either crevice or roughness. She felt again through the pigeonholes, pressing and prying in the hope that somewhere she might release a secret drawer; with each passing moment she became more frantic.

She scratched the last match and, in its raveling flare, she went once more through that clutter of papers. She stood up and her eyes, darting round in despair, abruptly paused in grim focus on the gilt-framed chromo of a voluptuous blonde basking in nude splendor on the wall above the desk.

Her gaze narrowed.

She was reaching for the picture, convinced the note was back of it, when her match flickered out. And at that precise instant, bent forward, still reaching, she caught the sudden rasp of a key being turned. She crouched there, frozen, incapable of movement, while the opening door flicked the wall with brief radiance. She whirled, eyes enormous, as the door was eased shut, leaving her in darkness through which the key turned again. And then soft steps started toward her.

BENDER in the doorway of the Three Brothers Hotel stood applying the sharpened end of a matchstick to divers particles of recalcitrant ham while trying to decide if he should go on to Deming or hurry back to Tres Pinos.

The note would have to be paid to clear the ranch of Lasham's hold on it but they still had more time to give to that chore than they had to get ready for a number of other things; and Krantz had promised to take delivery tomorrow, reminding Bender if the tally proved short he would expect the return of a proportionate amount of what he'd paid for the herd. The man had gone to the bank with him less than an hour ago and Bender had opened a ranch account for Don Leo, putting every nickel of the sale price into it. Although tempted to include that forty-five hundred he had finally gone to breakfast with it still in his pocket.

Yes, he thought, he'd be smart right now to get back to the ranch for, in addition to the need of making sure the herd was ready, there was always the chance Hazel's rifle-packing Yaquis might try to move in the sheep ahead of the deadline.

He picked up his horse and set off with a nagging disquiet at the back of his mind. His right arm, though not stiff, was almighty painful and he didn't have to move it much to feel its sharp protest. This was another of the reasons he'd decided against Deming; he was certainly in no shape to have to draw against experts.

He struck up a fast lope and was ten miles out and at the fork of the trail which ran north toward Cambray and Deming, with Mt. Riley well hidden behind the crags of the Potrillos, when he briefly debated swinging north after all.

That goddam note was a burden on his mind; but common sense prevailed and he kept on toward Tres Pinos.

Since he hadn't yet freed the crew of that herd, and couldn't until Krantz arrived to take delivery, he thought it might be better if he had the herd fetched down and either concentrated in the canyon itself or bedded at the foot of the bluffs. This would make the crew available in case of trouble with the sheep, and that many head of bawling horn-tossing cattle could be employed as a wall against invasion should Red Hat's crew of Yaquis attempt immediate entrance. With three thousand cattle he could choke the trail plumb solid where it ran along the base of the cliff in its ascent toward Three Pines' headquarters.

As a defensive measure this looked better than strychnine. For as long, at any rate, as they still had the cattle. And after that he'd have the crew. With *vaqueros* and *mozos* blended into one outfit dug in among the pines where the trail pinched in as it climbed through the bluffs, he should be able to make quite a dent in any invasion.

The more he now considered it the less inclined he felt toward using that strychnine. Barbed wire entanglements snarled across the trail should prove even more effective, and wire wouldn't hurt the range. In fact, so far as that went, now that the expectation of poison had been so firmly planted in the minds of the sheep crowd, common flour scattered around should be just as efficacious.

He couldn't help but feel events might be taking a turn for the better. With the discovery of Krantz and the sale of the cattle he now had a fighing chance to beat Lasham, to keep him at least from overrunning Tres Pinos. The ranch and Don Leo were still up against it but the future didn't look quite as dark as he'd imagined it. He hadn't netted too much from the sale of that herd but what he'd got was better than having it stampeded or stolen. Only one thing could wreck that part of the set up—the appearance of Chesseldine in advance of Krantz's coming. That, he thought, scowling, would screw the works proper.

He raked a swift look around. They were now quartering

along the southern footslopes of the Potrillos and somewhere along about here, he remembered, was that little-used
trail he'd seen angling northeast. He didn't believe Syd Hazel
could have brought up the sheep yet but, in the event Syd
had, their presence, even if unchallenged, might very well
have closed the south trail to travel. He couldn't afford to risk
it if there were another way in. It might take him a little
longer to reach Tres Pinos through these mountains, but sometimes the longest way around was the shortest. Red Hat wasn't
the man to forget that smashed elbow or to overlook any
opportunities for ambush.

Bender found the dim trace and turned his mount into it.
He knew it might turn out to be nothing more than a rabbit
run, but if he'd calculated right and this was actually some
long-abandoned way through the mountains, it should bring
him out somewhere between the Lopez ranch headquarters
and the lake Don Leo had offered him before the loss of the
lease lands had cancelled that deal.

The terrain became increasingly more difficult to negotiate.
At times the route became completely impassable, choked and
lost in patch after patch of pear and chaparral; at other places
it was strewn with rock rubble and cut away by gullies. It was
a nightmare trail, if trail it ever had been, and when, still
climbing, he rode an hour later about the base of a towering
butte of red rock and found himself immobilized on the rim
of a precipice, he cursed in bitter outrage. He could see nothing in front of him but turquoise sky.

He got down off his horse with the wind flapping at him and,
dropping to hands and knees, peered over the edge. He almost
lost his breakfast. What looked to be the green of blobs of
brush far below him were unquestionably the tops of two-
hundred-foot pines. But this wasn't the sheer drop he had
first supposed it. A kind of natural ladder led down the face
of this fault. Great blocks of rock showed sunlit slants from
which gnarled junipers occasionally lifted and the pagan shapes
of flowering *sotol;* shattered cliffs and tangles of catclaw; talus
and shale and, far below in dreamlike splendor the octagonal

outline of a forgotten valley slumbering in the bosom of rolling sugarloaf hills.

Bender drew back to catch his breath and give his stomach time to right itself. It staggered belief to think that even a goat could find a way down, yet graven on the rock between his white-knuckled hands were the unmistakable marks of shod hoofs. And not all of these were old marks. There was one, streaked with metal, obviously made within the month. He knew then how Robinson Crusoe must have felt discovering his footstep.

When his heart quit thumping his gullet he peered over the brink again and, this time, saw Don Leo's *casa* like a tiny white box against a fold in the hills and, beyond it, dun and vast, the broad expanse of the desert. There was one lighter patch, a yellowish blaze, which he knew for dust and this, he concluded, was probably made by Lasham's sheep. By calculating the distance between the *casa* and the desert he estimated the sheep were still ten miles to the south of the bluffs.

He studied this dust patch carefully. It was no little flock Red Hat's Yaquis were moving. All the sheep Lasham owned must be under that dust and, if he willed it, the vanguard could be threatening Tres Pinos within a matter of hours; tomorrow night at the latest.

His guts turned cold and crawled at the thought of tackling the formidable descent to that valley, but time was suddenly become too precious to waste the span that would be required to go back. Clenching his jaws, he picked up the reins and stepped onto the two-foot ledge leading downward, narrowed eyes on his footing, a prayer in his heart.

At the ranch, Don Leo was opening the letter which Bender's hired gun hand had fetched with him from Deming. With Stroad left in charge of the trail-guarding *mozos* the old man had jogged up to the *casa* for lunch and now, having eaten, he'd remembered the thing, having carried it forgotten overnight in his pocket.

The name on the envelope lightened his spirits. Postmarked

Santa Fe, this had come from Don Ramon Eusebio de Vega, his good friend who was in politics and might conceivably therefore have some weight with Otero. Don Leo had written suggesting the removal of Cash Fentress from the shrievalty and felt a comfortable satisfaction in the prospect of his friend's enclosed assurances.

The letter, however, contained little beyond proof of Deef Lasham's vast influence. Don Ramon, it appeared, had lost the governor's ear. Strange forces were at work in the land, he reported, and corruption had its tentacles in every department. He'd be extraordinarily lucky to retain his own post for its normal duration. He was sorry but there was nothing he could do. Sheriff Fentress, for the present, was entirely beyond his reach.

WHEN Bender reached the valley floor he dropped exhausted in the sunlit sand and lay there shaking like a man with malaria. His face was white as paper. The blue shield-fronted shirt, reflecting the hazards of his experience, was glued to his back with sweat. And when he finally arose and looked back up he could hardly believe he had actually made it.

He climbed into the saddle, too bone-weary to do much more than hold the gelding to its course. Landmarks looked different from this perspective and he had considerable difficulty in picking out the things he had decided on to guide him, but he knew the general direction.

He rode quietly along, nursing his luck, and after about thirty minutes came into a region of scraggly looking brush, which struck him as odd because, when he had been looking this country over before that climb down the face of that bugger of a precipice, he had seen the glint of water and, according to the way those yonder hills were shaping up, it had ought to be somewhere right along about here.

He had, in fact, been rather counting on it. There was no water bag on his saddle and he was drier than jerked buffalo. The more he thought about it the drier he got; and then, com-

ing over a low rise, he saw it, a short hundred yards ahead
of him.

He thought it uncommon odd his horse didn't have his
head up a-sniffing, was so indifferent as to have to be guided
toward it. But the horse was smarter than he was, as he
grudgingly admitted when he came to the pond's edge. No
wonder nothing grew there. It was the stinkingest water he
had ever got a look at; and one look was plenty. He didn't
even bother getting out of the saddle. He wheeled his horse
and headed straight for the hills.

He knew before he'd got over the first one he probably
wasn't going to be able to make it in time. The sounds he
had heard weren't made by any sheep and already the distant
clatter of gunfire had become sporadic, sure indication of a
running fight. He raked the big gelding's sides with his rowels,
flinging him headlong through rocks and brush. A running
fight could only mean one thing—that the herd was in motion.

And that meant Chesseldine.

19 | TOUCH AND GO

RUSTLERS, as a general rule, were prone to work under
the cover of darkness, drifting off small jags of stock, seldom
revealing the enterprise and brashness required to make off
with an entire herd. That Chesseldine now should do so—
and do it openly and boldly in the broad light of day—was
practical proof of a tie-up with Lasham and, more significant,
left little doubt but that the sheep king had abandoned all intention of further waiting.

Deef Lasham was a master of strategy. He always dovetailed
his efforts with meticulous planning so that when he employed
elements outside the law the goal was so nearly within his

grasp that, when the smoke rolled away, there was no one left to tattle. Obviously then, timed to coincide with this minor coup which was pulling away the bulk of Three Pines' defenders, others in Lasham's employ would be rushing up the sheep to take advantage of this distraction.

No one man was going to head those cattle now; if Gonzales with the crew couldn't get the herd stopped there was nothing Bender's presence on the scene could hope to accomplish.

It was hard, bitter hard, to see his work with Krantz undone—to contemplate having to return Krantz's money, but this was out of his hands now, beyond his power to circumvent. And already he had made one howling blunder in jumping to the conclusion it was grass Lasham was after. Sure, the sheep king *was* after grass—no doubt about it; but the paramount goal of all his scheming had nothing whatever to do with grass. It depended primarily on his acquirement of Three Pines.

So why hadn't he sat back and waited a little longer? Why resort to open violence, which was bound to necessitate the addition of still further violence to cover it, when by waiting another four and a half more days, and making certain that note was still unpaid, he could have had the place lock, stock and barrel?

Bender slowed and abruptly stopped his horse. Obviously something must have changed Lasham's plans, something crucial, something dangerous, something incredibly alarming. Only fright could have pushed the man into taking such risks. Fright and a terrible need for haste.

That confession may have done it combined with the knowledge Don Leo now possessed the funds to pay himself out. Whatever it was, Lasham had laid himself wide open and, if they could stand off the sheep. . . .

Bender turned the horse southeast again and lifted him into a larruping run. He had just remembered where he'd seen that damned gunfighter. *Stroad was the man whose horse he'd shot down on that ridge below the pines the night Fentress' posse had been after him!*

HEADQUARTERS looked deserted when Bender pulled up beside the *casa's* long gallery. He found Josefa in the kitchen, asked for Don Leo and was told the *patron* was at the shack on the bluffs. Everyone was there, all the servants, except one, too old and crippled, who'd been left at the stables to take care of the horses. "Well, see if you can scrape me up something to eat," Bender said, and went into the patio, heading for the *parada*.

He found the old man cleaning stalls and sent him off on a horse to fetch back Don Leo and Jose Maria. "But Jose, *senor*, is cowboy. He will be with—"

"Have him bring someone else then and hurry it up."

Giving the barrel a wide berth he cut across to his room, hastily washed and went back to the kitchen. There was a big plate of beans and a stack of *tortillas* on the table together with a graniteware pot of black and very hot coffee. Bender lost no time in pulling up a chair.

All the time he was eating his thoughts kept busy. When he'd wiped his plate clean and finished the last of the coffee he got out the makings and shaped up a smoke, wishing to hell his damn arm would quit hurting. "The *senorita*—where is she?" he asked, stepping over to the stove for a handful of matches.

The old woman straightened up. She put a hand to her *reboso*. "You have not heard? She went yesterday to Deming with the wagon for supplies—"

"Where is she now?"

"*Quien sabe?* She has not returned."

"Not returned!" Bender stared, and cold fingers turned over the food in his stomach. "Are you sure?"

"*Si*." The woman crossed herself. "The *patron*—he is like the madman."

He had reason to be, Bender told himself bitterly. Few things in this world could have suited Lasham better than to get hold of Blanca. With her for a hostage. . . .

WITH his shattered right elbow encased in a cast, the ubiquitous Syd Hazel lacked considerable of looking as tough as was his habit as he climbed the bluffs trail along with Fentress and three hard-faced Yaquis cradling rifles across their laps.

He'd encountered little difficulty in persuading the sheriff to pin a badge on his shirt. The lawman was glad of all the help he could get and he still looked like he was about set to vomit. As they were reining their horses toward the trees about the cabin Red Hat slanched a sideways look at the bastard and twisted his lips in a grimace of contempt. That goddam rep Lasham had hand-carved for Bender, plus the fellow's recent warning, had so worked on the sheriff through a long night of thinking that with the ghost of an excuse he would have funked the whole deal.

"You've hit the end of the line, *compadres*. Just turn them nags around now an' start back."

There was no one in sight but Hazel's narrowed eyes discerned the glint of several rifles. The sheriff had seen them too and his cheeks had turned a fish-belly white. He shot a scared look at Red Hat and stiffened enough to bluster: "You can't stop people here—this is a public road!"

"Try it on an' we'll find out."

"You're talkin' to the sheriff of this county," Fentress quavered.

A broken-nosed fellow with ears like a bat stepped out from behind the bole of a pine. There was a battered old hat pushed back off his forehead and a high-powered repeater in the crook of one arm. With a twist of his mouth he loosed a stream of tobacco juice. "This here's private property, gents, an' I've just been give orders to keep it that way." He regarded Fentress with a snaggle-toothed grin. "If you're a sure-enough sheriff let's have a look at your warrant."

Red Hat, scowling, made a project of wrapping the reins round his pommel. "Show it to him," he said; and half the curious *mozos* got up and stood gawping, muskets loose-hanging from pudgy brown fists. "Go ahead—let him read it. He's got a passion fer papers."

Stroad said, "You know how far you'll git with this, Hazel."

"Hell, it's no skin off my nose. He's the boss—we're jest

deppities. Go ahead an' stop him if you think you got a right to."

Fentress, having no warrant, didn't grasp any part of this but, under the compulsion of Hazel's iron stare, he put a rummaging hand to his coat's inside pocket, finally withdrawing a folded paper which he held out toward Stroad.

"I don't know what you think this'll buy you," Stroad said, looking hard at the sheep boss.

Red Hat grinned smugly, commenced unwrapping his reins as though this business of the warrant was a cut-and-dried sequence whose conclusion was so assured he had no need even to watch it.

Stroad snorted and stepped forward to have his look at the sheriff's paper. Swift as the strike of a snake Red Hat's hand swung saddleward and levelled, spouting flame.

Bender's gunfighter probably never knew what struck him. He spun half around with his mouth wide open, shuddered once and collapsed.

For an eternity of moments Bender stood without movement, oppressed by an overwhelming sense of futility.

He'd been an inexcusable fool—and worse—ever to have let these people start hoping he might be able to help them. Any two-year-old in diapers should have had the wit to understand once Lasham's toils closed round you there was nothing left but squirming. The man had too much influence, too much fire power, too much cunning. Each new shuffle of the cards had but served to strengthen this inescapable conviction. And on top of everything else, by God, from the instant he'd got into this thing, every move he'd made had been slapped around and bludgeoned by this girl's continual interference.

He heaved a sigh and got moving. No matter how badly he might be needed right here to cope with Syd Hazel, the sheep and Syd's Yaquis, the paramount issue right now was Blanca. They might stand off the sheep, they might beat the damn Yaquis, but so long as Deef Lasham had Blanca they were licked.

He remembered the confession but realized it was worthless. It would only give Lasham a belly laugh should he presume to offer it in exchange for the girl. It had been a real threat when he'd made the sheep king sign it but he had scrapped every vestige of a chance to use it by returning to Tres Pinos. A deep and hard-fought knowledge of Lasham's methods convinced him that by now every trail leading out of this region would be closed. Very probably he wouldn't even be able to get to Deming, but he had to make the try.

It would require a stout horse and a fast one.

The supply had been depleted by the need of mounting the *mozos*. What were left would likely be culls, he thought, moving through the passage and into the *parada*. His glance swept the stalls, abruptly focused on a dun. He hurried forward. It was Chucho!

He caught up the nearest saddle, grabbed a bridle off a wall peg; he was hastening toward Chucho's stall when the sound of horses twisted his head and hung him there, moveless, until Don Leo's voice gave him back mobility.

He had barely got Chucho readied when the *ranchero*, followed by a pockmarked *mozo*, came bursting into the stableyard. The don's face had aged ten years and anguish rode the flash of his stare, but it was Bender who got the first words out: "I know—I'm going after her. Put this fellow to work right away. Have him tangle barbed wire all across that trail where it comes up from the bluffs—"

"But we have already put out the poison—"

"Nothing but barbed wire's going to stop those sheep, and you've got to stop those Yaquis as well. Spread all the loose wire you've got down there and make sure it's well anchored along both sides. Post your *mozos* in cover and tell them to drop every Yaqui they see."

"But, *amigo*—"

"But—hell! You ain't goin' to hurt them snappin' a saddle blanket at them! You got to grind that soft stuff out of your system—you can't fight that kind with charity! You—" He pulled his head up, listening. "Was that a shot?"

TRES PINOS' servants, in terror of the red-hatted *gringo,* threw down their old-fashioned muskets with faces blanched to the color of putty. Several of the more devout hastily made the sign of the cross, others stood goggling; two, more hardy than the rank and file, would have bolted forthwith had not Hazel's gun suddenly swung to cover them.

"Round 'em up," he grunted, and the Yaquis got busy.

Inside of five minutes every *mozo* was bound and piled up like stove wood out of sight in the shack. Leaving one of his Yaquis to make sure they stayed put, the sheep boss and Fentress and the other pair pushed on.

They were almost in sight of the *casa* before the sheriff recovered his power of speech. After two or three stammering starts he blurted: "Hadn't we oughta made sure that feller was done for?"

Red Hat spat, not bothering to answer.

DON LEO shook his head. "I did not hear anything."

Bender listened a couple moments longer, then turned with a shrug and picked up Chucho's reins. He guessed he had better get started. He recalled Blanca saying that any shots at the shack were easily heard here, so perhaps after all he'd just imagined the sound; in any event it had not been repeated. If there'd been trouble at the bluffs it wouldn't have been wiped out with one bullet.

"I don't know what I'll be up against—I may not get through; but while I'm gone," he said bluntly, "you watch that trail as though your life depended on it. You," he told the *mozo,* "go scout up that wire—*andale. Pronto!*"

He watched the man go hurrying off.

"You can arrange with Josefa about the food. Have it sent down. String all the wire you can get hold of. Leave it tangled and loose but anchor it solid at the sides. Scatter your men around through those pines and see to it that everyone keeps his eyes skinned. At the first sign of trouble start blasting— don't hesitate. Understand?"

Don Leo nodded.

But he didn't, to Bender, appear sufficiently impressed. He

was too obviously engrossed with his worries about Blanca. In an effort to get through to him, Bender said, "You're up against a man who's playing for high stakes. It's this ranch he's after and—"

He let the rest go, glance abruptly remote, head canted in absorbed attention. He had thought to have caught the dim flutter of hoofs but, though his every faculty strained to recapture it, he heard nothing beyond the pawing of the impatient Chucho. A bot fly droned through the sunlit quiet and the restive animal snapped bared teeth. Then, as Bender would have spoken, the crash of a rifle locked his glance with Don Leo's.

One instant they stood, like robot figures hacked from clay, chained motionless by their thoughts. Both faces, whipping around then, grimly focused toward the gallery.

"Damn!" Bender swore: and both of them lunged for the passage. The old man, in spite of his age, managed to reach its entrance first. Crowding his heels Bender followed him into the patio and was halfway across it, rounding the bird bath, hurt arm cramped in a reach for his pistol, when a hoarse voice cried out back of them: *"Hold it!"*

20 | DEATH IN THE AFTERNOON

BENDER knew the full futility of all he'd tried to do here.

A sinking feeling that was like a physical weakness churned through his bowels as his bitter stare, back-flung across a shoulder, took in the ragged shape of the grinning Yaqui crouched in the passage behind a levelled Sharps. A thousand thoughts pounded through his head and he'd have probably gone on and dragged his own gun anyway but for the nearness

of Don Leo and the booted clank of spurs now coming toward
them from the house.

When he pulled his face around he saw Syd Hazel and the
sheriff and let the piled-up breath spill out of him. He felt
the sheep boss' eyes bite into him and stood slack-muscled
as Hazel, followed by Fentress, both with pistols in their hands,
stepped around the fountain.

Hazel, sneering, stopped less than two feet away from
him. "Unbuckle your belt and drop it."

Had the sheriff, white-cheeked and patently scared enough
to shoot at the least provocation, not been quite so close, he
might have made an attempt to kick the gun from Hazel's fist.
It wasn't consideration of any personal danger which made
him discard the impulse, but the conviction that any resistance
now would get Blanca's father killed out of hand. The old
man had plenty of courage but he was certainly not fitted
to cope with renegades of this stripe. He wasn't even armed.

So he let the belt fall, hearing above the thud of his pistol
the audible sigh that came out of Cash Fentress. It was like
the sound of a pricked balloon and showed how tight the
man's nerves had been strung.

A hungry emptiness climbed into Bender's stomach.

He had heard that soldiers facing death were often brought
face to face with visions from their pasts, that drowning men
sometimes had the same experience; and he realized now how
apt were those descriptions. For superimposed against the sunlit yard upon the baleful malevolence of Red Hat's features
he saw a brief montage of himself in a hundred actions; all the
salient milestones of his life reeled past in the kaleidoscopic
shuffle of a couple of heartbeats. And then the past was gone,
sponged as figures from a slate, and he was facing Syd Hazel
across a pounding silence.

In the sultry brilliance of the man's vengeful stare he could
read the violent ultimate of the sheepman's berserk fury—
invited it by prodding him with a cold disdainful grin.

With a strangled snarl Red Hat struck him across the face
with his pistol—viciously, deliberately, with all the towering
strength of his outrage.

Staggering backward, half blinded, Bender retained the wit through all the racketing roar of monstrous pain crashing over him to guide his stumbling feet till he could fall where he'd intended. He had no consciousness of striking ground. Blue sky advanced and receded in pulsating waves of nausea. Don Leo's shocked and angry protest was a faroff whisper floating through miles of rust-colored murk, yet he clung doggedly to the sound of it, refusing to allow himself the luxury of oblivion. He must, his brain kept telling him, retain at least this toehold on reality lest all their lives be forfeit. He could not, *dared* not, pass out now . . . he had to get to Blanca.

He heard Syd Hazel's raging tones, a gasp, the wheeze of panting breath; and found himself on hands and knees. The world around him reeled and rocked on changing patterns of light and shadow. He got one foot planted under him and with a savage wrench of muscle lurched upright.

He saw them now, gyrating shapes that writhed and twisted like flames in hell—only these were black, grotesquely tangled, the grappling, cursing figures of men entwined in murderous scuffle. Even while his eyes strained to focus, one queer lop-sided shape spun free trailing a spume of foul invective. The words were a screech half strangled by rage but the voice that propelled them was unmistakably Hazel's. "Stand back, you fools, so I can spill out his guts!"

There was a flash, a roar, and Bender, knuckling blood and sweat from his eyes, saw Don Leo stagger out of the group and fall headlong. One limp outflung arm abruptly twitched and was still with its fingers dug into the sunlit sand. Hazel, the smoke still curling from the gun in his fist, looked around and found Bender. "I'll have that money now. *And* the paper!"

Bender stared at the man's reptilian eyes and knew why he wasn't being gunned out of hand. The sheep boss first had to make sure of that confession, had to see it and handle it before he dared let his rage have full play.

He came nearer, suspiciously watching Bender's hands go through his pockets. "Pitch 'em over," he growled from eight feet away.

Bender's vacuous gaze took in the other pair's placement. They had paused indecisively where Hazel had left them beyond the fountain, six feet back of Red Hat; closer to Bender's dropped shell belt than he was—too close for him to ever hope to get at it.

Yet he had one chance left, an exceedingly thin one, hardly the ghost of a chance really but the one he had angled for while taunting the sheepman into knocking him sprawling.

He creased the bills once again and with an aggravating slowness carefully folded the confession so the banknotes lay beneath it. There was no breeze blowing, though he felt the breath of one. The currency, of course, weighed more than the paper.

He started forward, hand out, and saw Hazel's gun shift. "You biddin' for a harp?"

The muzzle of the weapon looked big as a stovepipe.

Bender licked at his lips. "I thought you—"

"*Throw* it!" Red Hat snarled.

The edge of a smile flattened Bender's mouth for he had the man now exactly where he wanted him. The rest of this play was on the lap of the gods. He thought morosely of Don Leo and desperately of Blanca and a leaching chill crept into his blood; and then he made the throw. The banknotes landed at Red Hat's feet. The confession wabbled in the air and dropped, still twirling, into the barrel.

THE sheepman's eyes winnowed down to glittering slits. It seemed as though his swelling chest would burst in another instant. Then his breath came out in a rasping laugh that bore no relation to anything human. "Tricks again, eh? Tryin' to get at that barrel! Well, you're not foolin' *me!*"

He called up the Yaqui. "If he jiggles a finger put a slug through him—savvy?"

The black Indian showed his teeth in a grin.

Hazel, looking equally malevolent, moved to the barrel and, still watching Bender, laid his gun on the ground and reached for the paper.

His face went suddenly the color of wood ash. He sprang to his feet and peered into the barrel and his eyes looked like they would roll off his cheekbones. He stared at his hand with twisted cheeks while a terrible horror-filled scream tore out of him. Cash Fentress came dashing from back of the fountain. The Yaqui's head turned and Bender leaped.

A musket crashed from the kitchen doorway. The Indian staggered and Bender's hand scooped up Hazel's pistol. He and the sheriff fired almost in unison.

Fentress' shot whined over his head. Dust whacked out of the starpacker's coat and he took three backward lurching steps with his mouth stretched wide in a strangled yell. Bender's next shot knocked the Yaqui down. The rifle went clattering out of his grasp as Josefa, *rebozo* flapping across a wild eye, waddled toward the *patron* with her black skirts caught in a shaking hand.

Bender ran for the stableyard.

21 | "I'LL BE SAYIN' GOODBYE NOW"

LAMPS were being lighted as Bender rode into the outskirts of Deming. He had no idea where he might discover Lasham. He was well aware of the risk he would run in showing himself at the Aces Up but could think of no alternative. He had to find Lasham before the sheep king learned what had happened at Tres Pinos.

That he would learn, and swiftly, Bender could not doubt. The appearance of Red Hat with the sheriff and those Yaquis made it more than amply evident his trail block had been breached; Stroad, after all, must have been in the sheepman's pay.

Hazel, probably, had fetched up the bulk of his fighting

Yaquis and Don Leo's *mozos,* in the face of such force and that damned Stroad's defection, had been too frightened to offer any resistance. Someone, already, was surely packing the news to Lasham and, once the sheep king understood that the girl was now owner of Three Pines Ranch, he would take steps at once to protect his interests. He would find some way to make her sign the place over; then she would simply disappear.

This wouldn't be the first time such things had happened.

Consumed though he was by this terrible impatience, Bender had the good judgment to pull Chucho down before he entered the town. Anxious as he was to come to grips with the sheep king, to get at the final showdown, he was cool enough to know that he would first have to find him. He wasn't going to find him if someone shot him out of the saddle.

This day had been months in coming. He could afford to exercise enough care to get there. He had lived this accounting a thousand times in the light of the flames from his lonely campfires, perfecting each detail, polishing his remarks, enjoying the fright he would see in those bloating features. During all those days he'd been steadily pushed westward by Lasham's pet marshal he'd found time to get used to the feel of his fingers clamped around Lasham's windpipe—to revel in it and long for it. In his mind he had cold-bloodedly killed Deef Lasham times without number and found it easy as wringing the neck of a chicken. He could do it, all right, and pretty soon he was going to. Lasham's business with Blanca had become the final straw.

And he was all through trying to fool himself on that score. In spite of her exasperating ways, her present danger had shown him beyond all his angered attempts to doubt it that whatever it was he felt toward her it certainly wasn't hate. But even if he was fool enough to actually admit he cared for her, that would have to be the end of it; he sure wasn't going to go blurting it out after what he'd discovered about Tres Pinos!

He pulled up by the tie rack in front of the hash house next door to the place where he had smashed Hazel's elbow and dourly regarded the gold squares of its windows. If he went in there now and got the dope he was after and got out again, in a matter of moments he might be facing Deef Lasham. But if he went in there and didn't get it, or got killed in the process, what about Blanca?

But it was almost as risky being seen in this street. He felt a quick, tense excitement. Any one of this procession of ambling townsmen might glance up and chance to remember his profile. There'd been a lot of guys engaged in that shooting the other night; there had been several horses killed and a lot of glass broken, and the owners of these weren't like to forget him. Nor the owner of that horse he had finally got off on.

He watched three conversing punchers go past, their spurs dragging sound from the planks of the walk. Midway of the block they swung right and went into the Drovers Hotel. Another couple came along, a man and a woman. A dancehall girl by the look of her apparel.

Bender nudged his horse deeper into the blackness and asked gruffly if they knew where he might find a man named Lasham.

"Don't know 'im," the man said, but the girl's arm, acting like an anchor, swung him round. "What's he in—tobacco or whiskies?"

"Neither," Bender said, "he's a sheepman," and could see the pale blob of her face peering up at him. Her companion snorted and tried to pull her along, but she got hold of the tie rail. "Wait a minute, Joe. I wanta talk to this john—"

"You don't want no truck with a—"

"He's no sheepman," she muttered, and the man's head came round.

Bender eased Chucho back a bit and the man suddenly growled on an upswing of interest, "By cripes, I—"

"Get your hand off that gun," intoned Bender. "All I'm huntin' is a little information. You know where I can locate him?"

"If you mean the fat slob—"

"That's the one." Bender said.

"Anyone could tell you. He's sure been rollin' it—settin'

'em up for folks all over town. Got a flossy office in the Plaza of the Virgin. Gold paint on the window—Potrillo Sheep & Land Development. Open day an' night. I can't see how you missed it. Go eight blocks west and—"

"Gracie, you dimwit! This is the—"

"Now Joe, honey, don't get yourself all worked up about it. You don't know this gent. You just stick to your lovin' an' . . ."

BENDER tied his horse half a block up the side street, tugged down his hat and sauntered back toward the plaza. Under the board awning of the Caballo Colorado he propped himself against a post and fetched out the makings while his eyes ransacked the piled-up shadows behind the tan adobe housing Lasham's place of business. Might be a window or two back there but if there was you could bet it was covered. Deef Lasham hadn't set this stage to help Don Leo. The lamplit front of that office with the blinds clean up to the ceiling was sucker bait—same way with the people moving round inside it.

Bender hadn't ridden past the front of that place but he had got near enough to admire Deef Lasham's handiwork. Anyone who didn't know the way that scheming devil's mind worked wouldn't hesitate a minute. It was a trap though just the same—a cunning deadfall rigged for murder.

There was a fellow carefully blended with the shadows flanking the hardware shop who'd been very likely put there to take care of Three Pines' payment.

This bird was directly across the plaza where he could get a good look at anyone who went over there, hard to pick out in the gloom where he loitered. Anyone undertaking to pay their bills at that office was going to get the works if they came from Tres Pinos.

Just across the calle de la Piedad from where Bender stood before the Caballo Colorado there was a dark house whose left side flanked the back of that lamplit office. The girl was probably imprisoned in that house, tied hand and foot or locked into some room she had no chance of getting out of.

Lasham, too, was probably in there, hidden someplace in the felted blackness, watching to see if his trap would be sprung.

Bender chewed on his lip. To get into that house he'd have to cross this street, and it was a cinch when he tried that guy was going to start firing.

He was standing there, debating, when he caught the dim mutter of hoofs and knew he dared wait no longer.

He pasted the unlighted smoke on his lip and stepped away from the post. That fellow off yonder was harder to see now; like enough he'd stepped back where the gloom was piled deeper. Bender's heart banged around like a chained canary. He felt the cold sweat creeping out along his collar but he held his advance to a snail's pace till he was certain he'd got clear away from the saloon and had nothing behind him but solid night.

Now, drawing his gun, he moved in swiftly while the hoof sound got louder and he expected any moment to feel the impact of lead.

But the fellow didn't fire. He didn't try to bolt, either. He turned out, when Bender neared him, to be nothing more alarming than a stoop-shouldered peddler still pottering around his little pushcart of fruit.

Bender, wheeling disgustedly, was smothering an oath when some sixth sense made him throw a glance upward. He was barely in time to miss the rush of the bullet that came racketing at him from the store's sloping roof. The peddler took to his heels. Bender, lunging sideways and dropping as he did so, hammered three slugs at a sky-shrouded shape. The last one did it. He saw flailing arms as the man quit the roof.

The staccato of hoofs climbed into crescendo. Bender, ducking his head, punched shells from his pistol and with frantic fingers plugged the holes with fresh cartridges. Light from the front of Lasham's office thrust golden lanes into the square's black shadows but, with that oncoming rider less than three blocks away, there was no time to lose.

Bender tore across the plaza, plunging into the alley to the left of Lasham's office. Stumbling and lurching through tin cans and bottles, he scrambled up an embankment and

reached the clapboarded side of the dark house behind it. He
had one last moment of desperate wonder when the paralyz-
ing thought leaped fullblown through his mind that perhaps
once again the sheep king had outslicked him by somehow
hiding Blanca among the crowd in that office.

He tongued the unsmoked cigarette off his lip. He faced a
terrible choice. The girl's life might be lost if he guessed wrong
now—she might be spirited away while he was making his
mind up. But if he went into this house and she wasn't there.
. . . There simply wasn't time for him to look in both places
and the sound of that horse thundering into the plaza decided
him.

He turned left, cold with dread, and went up the back steps
of the house. He hit the door hard with the point of his
shoulder, took the splintered wood with him as he lunged into
a blackness that was rank with the smell of recently burned
tobacco. His knee struck a chair and sent it skittering through
darkness. His left, outstretched hand came against the slick
surface of a painted wall. He moved the hand along this and
with cocked muscles followed it through an unseen opening
into another room where the cigar smell was stronger and a
faint sound of breathing suddenly stopped him in his tracks.

Somewhere in this impenetrable blackness another shape
was also crouched, finger about trigger, eyes wide with staring,
ears straining in the agony of pinning sound to source.

He imagined he was confused by lack of sight when, after
holding himself completely doggo for many seconds, he still
was not sure where that breathing was coming from. He
would have sworn at first he'd caught the sound on his right,
then began to think it was more nearly in front of him, wind-
ing up half convinced it was off to his left. No man, even
bootless, could have shifted that rapidly without leaving evi-
dence in creaking boards and, when he realized this, Bender
had no choice but to conclude the room was packed.

One of these people might conceivably be Blanca but
neither his eyes nor his ears could tell him which one. It was
an intolerable situation, a deadlock which would only be

resolved when someone's nerves could stand the strain no longer and impelled him, or her, to suicidal movement.

And what if the first sound came from Blanca?

How could he know? How, indeed, dared he fire, *not* knowing.

The two matches Stroad had given him were still unused in the band of his hat and he turned this knowledge over while he wondered what had happened to the rider whose horse he had last heard entering the plaza. Where was that man now?

He remembered abruptly that the back door was open, splintered and sagging on twisted hinges. The night was too black for him to show up against it, but not too black for that mysterious rider to find the way in through its unguarded opening.

The thought brought its cold stir of air curling round him; and out of this pulsating nightmare of silence came the sibilant whisper of cloth brushing cloth.

Bender's heart started pounding and the stillness piled up and churned tighter and tighter. Like a lantern slide thrown on a sheet by projection he saw Toby Bronsen's white face as it had looked in that awful moment before buckling knees had dropped his dead flesh in the yellow dust. And then, through remembrance, through the brittle quiet of nerves stretched taut and the ghastly run of the dragging minutes, he caught the stealthy creep of movement.

No sound to put a name to. No scratch, no thump, no scrape or rustle. Not even enough to hold a hint of direction —a conviction rather. A presentiment of motion.

Bender held himself rigid, the sweat pouring out of him.

He couldn't maintain this position much longer. A muscle twitched in his jaw. His back felt as though it must snap any moment.

He put up his left hand to get hold of the matches. But a deep and hard-bought knowledge of danger warned him not to pull them out of the band. The rasp of their sticks against the felt of his hat would be all the sound needed to send hammers against cartridges. He pushed the hand higher and, with an infinite patience, worked the hat off his head and braced his body to toss it.

He was like that, waiting in the stance of Discobolus, when knuckles rapped loudly against the front door.

Muzzle light leaped across the blackness in front of him and Bender, clapping on his hat, ripped a slug through it frantically and struck the floor, rolling, as another sixgun loosed a livid flash from the left. He felt the shock of the bullets tearing through the thin planking. Somewhere in the pounding din a man's lifted scream dropped away to a gurgle. The explosions' pulsations beat against the walls like sledges and he fired three more times and jumped erect, coldly waiting through that swirling stench of powder to throw in a final shot.

Lasham's cracked voice groaned, "I've got enough. Don't fire—I'll throw my gun down."

Bender heard it thump the floor. He neither spoke nor moved, just waited.

"I—I'll strike a light," Deef Lasham quavered.

A match flared in the sheep king's fist. His monstrous shadow climbed the walls. Bender's glance flicked once to Blanca's face then watched the fat man light a lamp and, when its yellow glow spread round, saw the Yaqui's dead sprawled shape six feet away and wondered how the man had passed him. Not that it much mattered.

Weariness bowed his shoulders and reaction was like a cold lump in his belly. He looked at the cowering hulk that was Lasham and all he could feel was a tired contempt.

He dropped the gun in his holster. Gagged and lashed in a chair by the splintered desk Blanca's eyes were like crazy. Like usual, he reckoned, she was bursting to get in her two-bits worth of talk and having a hemorrhage because he didn't move faster.

He threw a glance round the room, noting the blanket covered windows, the blanket-draped chair in the room's far right corner, the dead Indian, the gross bulk of Deef Lasham standing back of the desk.

There was something about the man's shaved-hog features which seemed not quite in keeping with his air of resigned deflation. But when he looked for and found the sheep king's dropped pistol, shoved it off to one side and hazed him back from the desk, Bender felt free to give his mind to the girl.

Now the danger was over he could think of Blanca more dispassionately and was able to persuade himself it was probably just as well she hadn't guessed his true feelings. They'd been too differently reared—would have clashed every whipstitch. Bound to. They were opposites in everything, with the additional barriers of race and temperament. Mexican and Texican. The two just didn't go together.

Smothering a sigh he shook his head and moved toward her.

Her eyes wigwagged at him with frantic desperation; but it was the glint he caught in Lasham's that wheeled him just as gun's thunder jumped the flame of the lamp up. A second shot crowded it so close as to be inseparable, and Chesseldine staggered from behind the draped chair, spun half around and folded.

Stroad in his sockfeet, with a gun in his hand and a badge on the front of his blood-stained shirt, came out of that dark back room, toughly grinning.

Bender understood then. "Lasham's pet marshal!" he said, and passed out.

When he opened his eyes he found his head in Blanca's lap and her white frightened face bending over his own. "Don't die—please don't die," she said and Stroad, inelegantly, back of them snorted.

"Never heard of anyone dyin' yet from a .44 slug goin' through the wrong shoulder—that Art was a helluva shot," he said critically. He came around and looked down. "Just hold the bandage right where I put it till the doc gits back—that was him you folks heard knockin'. He'll be round soon's he's satisfied the fireworks is over."

Bender said, "Where's Lasham?" and in the same breath allowed he felt able to sit up, but the marshal opined he'd better let well enough alone.

"You're in good hands," he winked, "and I've got that fine sheepman all taken care of. I'd already had me a talk with

Bronsen that mornin' afore he got knocked off; so when Lasham come along, figurin' to buy himself a lawman, I acted the underpaid public servant an' let him talk me into pushin' you west'ard."

Stroad grinned. "Figured if I give the old goat enough rope he'd save me a lot of trouble, an' he did. There's one thing about crooks—they ain't never so slick as they make theirselfs out to be.

"I hear the doc comin', so I'll let you tell Miz Blanca what it was them birds was after. She knows about her Dad an' about Gonzales savin' the cattle. Hazel's dead an'—he was another rotten shot!—Cash Fentress will live to learn the error of his ways. I got that confession. Likewise a bankroll; so don't either of you get to frettin' about that note. I'll see it's taken care of an', by this time tomorrer, I'll have them sheep an' Lasham well on the way to Texas where that bustard will be lucky if he don't git his neck broke. I'll be sayin' goodbye now—you take care of that young lady."

Bender sighed and Blanca looked at him anxiously. He could see she had been crying—probably worked up over her father. Not knowing what else there was he could say, he told her about Tres Pinos, about that pond in the valley he'd found at the foot of the precipice. "There's oil under there. That's what Lasham was after. You won't have to be worryin' about payin' your hands off, or the cost of more range or anything else now. You'll be richer than Croesus—"

"No!" Blanca said. "That land is yours. My father gave it to you."

"That deal was called off—"

"By you, perhaps. Never by us. When we give to someone something we do not take it back—ever." She turned her face away stubbornly. "Do not anger my father's memory. The land is yours."

"Very well," Bender said. "But after we get married—"

The change in her face was amazing.

"Oh—*querido!*" she cried and Stroad, softly chuckling, tramped down the steps and departed.